Other Books by Wayne Karlin

Crossover
Lost Armies
The Extras
Us
Rumors and Stones: A Journey

As editor:

Free Fire Zone: Short Stories by Vietnam Veterans (contributor
    and co-editor with Basil T. Paquet and Larry Rottmann)
*The Other Side of Heaven: Postwar Fiction by Vietnamese and
    American Writers* (contributor and co-editor with Le Minh
    Khue and Truong Vu)
Truan ngan My duong dai (*Contemporary American Short
    Stories*), (contributor and co-editor with Ho Anh Thai)
The Stars, the Earth, the River: Short Fiction by Le Minh Khue
Behind the Red Mist: Short Fiction by Ho Anh Thai

Praise for *Prisoners*

"*Prisoners* is superb. The reader is drawn into this powerful, richly-layered novel by the poetic language, the compelling stories, and the wide-ranging themes. Ultimately we realize the various ways we are all prisoners of war."—Bobbie Ann Mason

"Wayne Karlin's skilled literary fingers have woven from many disparate threads a stunning tapestry. It is at once infuriating, enlightening, inspiring, creative and forgiving—reaching out to touch a very real peace. Mother Teresa said, 'if we have no peace, it is because we have forgotten that we belong to each other.' Wayne Karlin has, with *Prisoners*, reminded us that we belong to each other."—Lynda Van Devanter, author of *Home Before Morning: The Story of an Army Nurse in Vietnam*

"*Prisoners* is the kind of novel which tells the rest of us what fiction can do when it is at its very best."— Fred D'Aguiar, winner of the Whitbread Prize for *The Longest Memory*

"This complicated, highly textured novel attempts exploration of one of the deepest and most painful questions concerning the watershed American theme: race relations. *Prisoners* becomes an original look at our increasingly incomprehensible country."—*Multicultural Review*

PRISONERS

a novel
by
WAYNE KARLIN

CURBSTONE PRESS

All characters in this novel are fictitious. Any resemblance to individuals, living or dead, is purely accidental.

Printed in the U.S. on acid-free paper by Sheridan Books

Curbstone Press is a 501(c)(3) nonprofit literary arts organization whose operations are supported in part by private donations and by grants from foundations. In the past year support was received from the Connecticut Commission on the Arts, the Connecticut Arts Endowment Fund, the Connecticut Humanities Council, Lawson Valentine Foundation, the National Endowment for the Arts, the Puffin Foundation, the Samuel Rubin Foundation, and the Soros Foundation's Open Society Institute.

Our sincere thanks to Matthew Proser, Jane Blanshard, Barbara Rosen, Molly Stephanou, Ellen Partridge and Lisa Farino.

Library of Congress Cataloging-in-Publication Data

Karlin, Wayne.
    Prisoners : a novel / by Wayne Karlin.
        p.   cm.
    ISBN (cloth) 1-880684-56-X
    ISBN (paperback) 1-880684-71-3
    1. Vietnamese conflict, 1961-1975 — Veterans — Maryland
    — Fiction. 2. Point Lookout Prison Camp for Confederates
    — Fiction. I. Title.
    PS3561.A625P75   1998
    813'. 54—dc21   98-20553

published by
CURBSTONE PRESS   321 Jackson Street   Willimantic, CT 06226-1738
        phone: (860) 423-5110   e-mail: books@curbstone.org
                    www.curbstone.org

Acknowledgements

Several sections of this book, in different versions, have appeared in various publications, including *Crab Orchard Review, Indiana Review, Prairie Schooner, Tac Phom Moi and Tuoi Tre (in translation, Viet Nam), Vietnam Generation*; and anthologized in *New Fiction from the South: The Best of 1993; The Other Side of Heaven: Postwar Fiction by Vietnamese and American Writers;* and *The Vietnam War in American Stories, Songs and Poems.*

White gauze curtains
sift a cold sunrise.
A dust of broken surface,
a weave of March light,
pile the edges of marble.
Stone defines a space
on a gouged wood bench.
He sits with his night's work,
working his palms across his knees.
Chipped fingers shift a tool.
He spits, rubs his hands
across the heaving surface,
darkening its grain to life.
Even now he sees the unborn child.
He holds his hands like secrets,
offering their legend to his stone,
humped bamboo finger joints,
palm lines forking like delta rivers.
He squeezes shut a fist of memory
and lays it on the stretched lip of his yawn.
His eyes tear with sleep,
glazing the long question of the stone
in its morning light.
A voice escapes the radiator
in tired whispers of steam
pressing toward his face,
the huts are afire, the well filled,
blue smoke pillars the sky,
hysterical cries of children
shake the corrugated tin.

He holds his stone,
its weight pulls him to the present;
the long shame of his war years
is deep and aching as a wound,
his deeper shame is knowing
he pities himself for remembering,
the smallness of it the unbearable stench
of his own unhealed corruption.
White curtains hold the morning sun,
villagers dance on the gauze screen
He joins them in their circle of light.
We are one! We are one!
Fingers feel voices in the stone,
the studio's quiet breathes in his ears.
He touches the blind stone,
shape of his deepest will,
a truth there in memory,
where he was the terror in their lives,
his hands ache to create beauty.

From "Ceremony of Souls"
Basil T. Paquet

i am accused of attending to the past
as if i made it
as if i sculpted it
with my own hand. i did not.
this past was waiting for me
when i came,
a monstrous unnamed baby,
and i with my mother's itch
took it to breast
and named it
History.
she is more human now,
learning languages everyday,
remembering faces, names and dates.
when she is strong enough to travel
on her own, beware, she will.

Lucille Clifton

PRISONERS

OCTOBER - NOVEMBER
1990

POINT LOOKOUT

MARY HAD JUST GOTTEN to work at midnight when the first gunshot casualty was brought in, the ambulance attendants nearly knocking her over in the corridor. She glanced down briefly and the boy's eyes met hers; he was fluttering somewhere in the pull between panic and unconsciousness. The boy was black, maybe fifteen; the wound was through the left chest wall.

Dr. Sayed grabbed her arm. "Give me a hand here."

She tried to walk past him. "I'm an obstetrics nurse, doctor."

"You're a fucking nurse, give me a fucking hand."

The double doors flung open and she saw another kid being wheeled in, clutching his belly.

She helped cut the rest of the boy's clothing off, got an IV going. The boy's eyes rolled back; he was making gargling noises. "Come on, for fuck's sake," Sayed said. They rolled the boy onto his right side and tied off the bleeders as Sayed cut, her hands falling into a rhythm she'd thought they'd forgotten. The doors slammed open again. Out of the corner of her eye she saw another child wheeled in, his hand clutching an Orioles' baseball cap. More doctors and nurses had arrived now, but it was a weekday night and they were a small country hospital and she knew she couldn't leave. Sayed removed a bullet from the boy they were working on and held it up for her to see. "7.62 millimeter," he said bitterly. "Where the fuck are we, nurse?" She helped start a saline irrigation. Sayed's hawkish brown face

1

seemed enclosed in a trance, as if the memory of another life had taken him over. She held ribs apart with a retractor. She helped get the chest tubes in to drain the wound, pump up his collapsed lungs; she catheterized the boy with difficulty, his penis shrinking as she tried to hold it. The floor was slippery with blood. "Hardee's restaurant," someone said, "guy just walked in." She wondered if Sayed had treated casualties of the Afghanistan war. She wondered where he'd learned to say fuck. The word, as had the movements of her own hands, called another memory, the way that particular word rolled out like someone screaming a panicky instruction when the death got too thick. She realized she couldn't remember if this observation had been hers from the time she'd worked ER or if she'd heard it from her husband. Sayed closed. She moved over with him, her feet sliding out from under her on the blood, helped debride the other kid's abdominal wound. It was embedded with what looked like pieces of a salt shaker; undigested hamburger and pickles were scattered up from the bowel to the chest. Her husband had been in a helicopter crew in the Vietnam war; he'd told her how during medevacs they'd pack the interior with wounded and dead, how the blood of the dead and living would mingle. At what point had their memories leaked together? Sponging, watching Sayed's skilled hands, his lean fingers squeeze along the length of a bowel, searching for fragments, probing, cutting, suturing skillfully, she felt a wave of lust, a heat that opened like liquid petals inside her body.

She didn't get to obstetrics until three in the morning. At eight o'clock, Margaret Vail, the shift supervisor, looked at her and told her to go home; she was calling in the standby nurse. No babies had been born on Mary's shift before she left. One of the three boys brought into ER had died. A man had walked into the restaurant—it was IHOP not Hardee's—and shot the black teenagers with cool deliberation. There were conflicting stories as to whether the man was black or white, if the shooting was part of a drug war or just the act of a crazy. She didn't ask Margaret if the shooter was a vet.

2

At home she vacuumed the living room and smoked. She waxed the kitchen floor. She did a load of laundry. Brian was at work and Zeke was in school. She couldn't stand the house. She made two pastrami on rye sandwiches and put them in a paper bag. When she went back out, the black Labrador, held on a running lead, whined at her piteously and even though she didn't like the dog, she unclipped him and let him jump into the back of the station wagon and she drove south to Point Lookout with him panting like the whole manic night behind her.

During the Civil War there had been a federal prisoner of war camp on the wedge of land between the Chesapeake Bay and the entrance to the Potomac; her husband was sinking trenches in a mass grave found south of Fort Lincoln, along the river shore. She parked in the recreation area parking lot and leashed Butch—the dog was young, too untrained to let loose at the site. The grass was shaded by tall loblolly pines, evenly spaced. She went under them, Butch pulling her into a half-run, to the sliver of beach, then turned and walked up it to the dig. There were virtually no waves on the Potomac side, though a breeze crinkled the surface of the river and a sparkling, transparent edge of the water advanced slightly on the sand beach then drew back to show a glittering strip of pebbles and shells.

Brian was hunched over a sifting tray. As she came up behind him she stood still for a moment, the movement of his fingers probing the sand reminding her of Sayed's.

Her husband looked up and smiled, his face registering confusion at seeing her there, reforming as it did when she'd wake him up from a dream.

"Mary? Everything all right?" he asked. "Down, Butch."

The dog was trying to jump up on him, trying to pull her arm from its socket.

"Sure," she said. She put her free arm around his waist. "I just felt like seeing you."

"Are you all right?" he repeated.

3

Several of the student volunteers were looking at her. One of them was wearing an Orioles' baseball hat. She closed her eyes tightly.

Brian hit the palms of his hands against his trousers. "Look, I need to finish here. Why don't you relax for a while, take a walk. We can do a picnic on the beach afterwards."

"Telepathy," she said. "I brought some sandwiches."

"I have..." he started to say, but something in her face must have stopped him. He squeezed her arm.

She nodded at the tray. "How's it going—any surprises?"

He looked distracted again. "Just dem bones."

He looked in fact worried, she thought with a sudden leap of her heart that startled her. The dig was grant funded and nearly finished—if Brian didn't find more burial sites or a more spectacular discovery, he didn't think there'd be any more money or a chance at a permanent teaching position at the college. Another archaeologist had found three lead coffins at the Historic State Capital site: they were believed to contain the remains of the founders of the state. Brian's dead Confederates couldn't compete. "They aren't politically correct corpses," he'd said bitterly, with an archaeologist's pride at finding and using a piece of contemporary language, an archaeologist's ignorance that the phrase was already somewhat dated. Her contempt surprised her. He wanted to buy the house they were renting here, and he thought she did too. She'd gone along with him in applying for the mortgage; it would be messy now if they had to move. But she'd just realized how relieved she'd felt when she'd seen the worry in his face. She didn't want to stay here.

She said she'd see him later.

The dog pulled her up the beach. She jerked sharply at the chain leash. "Heel, damn you." The dog looked back at her, all stupid Labrador affability, all wasted charm as far as she was concerned, and yanked her forward again. She pulled it to her, hand over hand, and at the end pulled up the collar, yanked the dog's forepaws right off the ground in a burst of rage. Butch panted and whined. She unclipped him and let him go. Maybe

4

the idiot animal would get lost. She felt suddenly ashamed of her anger though she recognized, another realization in the clarity of this morning's light, how deeply she disliked the dog. She could hear its panting, the relentless rustle of its pad keeping pace with her now, just behind the curtain of trees. Butch had been one of a litter born in the barn across the country street in front of their house; the puppies had swarmed the yard, Zeke and this one finding each other. "It's a pity for the kid to live in the country and not have a dog," Brian had said. But she had blown up at her son when she'd first heard him calling the puppy Butch, naming it, creating a responsibility, a living connection to this place, that she didn't want.

She stopped and squinted at the expanse of the river. She could barely see the coastline of Virginia; it was a misty gray line on the other side. On the Maryland side she could see up the green curve of the coast to the point of land which marked the head of the tributary that twisted in near the house: the Brits had sailed up here, turned there, began their settlement nearby, started something.

The dog came back, proudly holding a broken-necked rabbit in its mouth, its eyes gleaming over the broken flesh and fur. "You murdering little bastard," she said, and grabbed the hind quarters. The dog backed up, growling, digging its front paws into the sand, then snapping its head around and winning the tug of war, running off, its grinning mouth full of death.

She walked on towards the dig. Near or on this ground her feet pressed prisoners had starved to death or been murdered: Brian had found the pit he was working in an area where no dead were supposed to be; the corpses were thrown in haphazardly, some with shattered skulls, mini-balls buried in their bases; ribs splintered by bayonet thrusts. All of Point Lookout was supposed to be haunted: the locals had many ghost stories. Park rangers had picked up voices on recorders left out at night in deserted areas. She'd seen a photo taken during the sixties inside the Point Lookout lighthouse; when you stared at it long enough, a man in a Confederate uniform emerged from

5

the background. His face angry. His eyes accusing. Nothing went away. During their first year together she'd sometimes held Brian at night when he'd sweated and moaned, half suspecting it was phony, behavior copied from a movie or book, it seemed to her so much of the war was that anyway, but even if so the nightmares were there, the constant unearthing of the dead in his mind. She hadn't minded; they'd pull each other from the pit; whatever had been violated in him would leave a space where the flesh of their hearts could grow together: they would be closer in it than husband and wife, man and woman.

But they were in their twentieth year now and what had changed? A few weeks ago, Brian had been invited to go to Vietnam with a group helping to locate and bring home American remains from the war, still clenched as tightly as he was by that ground. And one of their neighbors, a counselor at a group residence for girls, had told her about a Vietnamese girl come into the program after being raped by her foster father; she'd been brought to the country as a baby, another maltreated remnant from the war, like the missing still haunting the Vietnamese jungles, or the vets she'd read about hiding in Oregon forests. Things that would not go away. Earlier in the year she'd miscarried (her mind going smooth and blank over the word) and the girl seemed somehow connected to the ache of loss she felt, she and her husband entwined in a curse whose elaborate intricacies wearied her. Brian suspected the miscarriage (it was a terrible word, truly, as if something inside her hadn't held the child right) might have had to do with his exposure to Agent Orange. But he wasn't sure how much exposure he'd had. That is to say he suspected a curse. Nothing went away. One night she'd come into his office to find him asleep at his desk, his desk light burning. By his hand were notes about the Point Lookout murders, under his sleeping head were photos and articles about My Lai that he was using as one of his modern references: the tangled and torn bodies of women and children pooled around his head like spilled dreams. Where the fuck are we, nurse?

She realized that her feet were getting wet. The ribbon of sand had gotten narrower: perhaps the tide was coming in. The water was icy. A red, clayey mud bank, maybe ten feet tall, grew up on her right side. The water had lapped and gnawed at it, created a dark cavern under a frozen Medusa spread of exposed and shiny tree roots. Butch was darting around the roots, barking. She saw him nose into the bank, his tail wagging, and begin to dig frantically, mud and water flying.

She called him and to her surprise he jumped into the water and swam over to her, making deep coughing and choking sounds; he had something gripped in his mouth. He got onto the sand and sat down and dropped it in front of her, a trick Zeke had taught him. She felt touched in spite of herself, more at seeing her son's efforts than at the dog's action. She reached for the slim brown cylinder, some part of her mind noting the shape, the knobbed ends, the cool, smooth almost plastic feel of it; as she touched it she felt a chill seizing over her skin. The dog growled and snatched it back, twisting it free. Butch ran off down the beach, then stood looking at her warily, the shape in its mouth like a cartoon cliche. From the size she thought it could be a femur.

She went to the umbrella of roots and tried to push herself in through two black, gnarled branches. The space was too narrow. She took off her shoes and waded out into the water, then squatted awkwardly and peered through the roots. At first it was too dim for her to be sure, but a shift of the light reflected off the waves, into the hollow worn in the fleshy clay bank, and in that second she could see a broken outline that she squinted and connected into a human form socketed into the clay: the washboard cage of the ribs, the pelvic cradle, the grin.

Brian, she'd seen him work, would photograph and sketch the site, plot the exact relationships of objects on a finely drawn grid: only then would he delicately brush the earth away, layer by layer. She reached both hands roughly into the opening between the roots and gripped and drew out as if to birth. The first one came loose with a wet, plopping sound, a satisfying release of tension. She placed it carefully on the sand—the dog had disappeared again—waded back and pulled out another, barnacle encrusted, cutting her hands, then another, then another, desecrating the site, leaving it torn and open. She tried to form the outline of a shape, lumping wet sand over the shapes, connecting. The water lapped dangerously close. She stood, feeling dizzy, and looked at what she'd placed on the beach, dem bones. But the form was incomplete, something strange and broken that had come from her. The hands were gone: there were too many parts missing; they left gaps, an aching void. And when she turned her head away again, the dog broke from the trees and snatched its trophy from her grasp.

THE LAST VC

"AND WHAT EXOTIC ISLE d'ye hail from?" the Union soldier asks me.

"Florida, mothafucka," I answer. The other girls crack up. The Union soldier has his act, I have mine. He's black and wears blue. I wear black. Other people dressed in history clothes parade back and forth on the grass. Me there to see the Ghost Tour with the other girls from Ruth's House, daffies, Disturbed Adolescent Females, the counselors think we don't know that label. Last week we went to Historic Maryland, saw the Founder's Ship, you can go aboard but nothing happens on it like Pirates of the Caribbean or anything, you just look at the sailors' hammocks and some barrels and go uh-huh. There wasn't much else. Just a visitor center looks like a barn and an inn (the dumb daffies singing we in the inn) and a brick building suppose to be the first capital, only the people looked around and said oh shit, the boonies, and left. That's it. Except for some little roped off places with signs telling you to believe that buried under the dirt is a tavern or a plantation or slave house or whatever they want to say is there. One little sign says trash midden: this window set into the ground like the glass bottom boat, what you see through it is four hundred years of dirty oyster shells and smashed up plates and cups, old chewed on bones. This garbage under everything.

"A saucy wench," the soldier say, winking at me. I give him my hooded, cool look, VCWA: Viet Cong With an Attitude, then

11

look away, staring around the area. Near the beach this big cannon, around it, on the lawn these white pyramid tents, camp fires, a fence made from long sharptop logs, everything blinking into existence as I look like the Star Trek holodeck where you can have any scene you want. For a minute I play with the scene being different for each group or individual that comes in, fitting these holes in their minds. I did a theme park, that's what it would be.

"K-K no saw-see 'xotic eye," Tonetta says to the Union, putting her palms on both sides of her head and pulling up the skin, tilting her eyes up, to show him what I am. "K-K jus a gook."

The other girls giggle, say gook, gook, like a flock of daffies, these disturbed dyslexiac-assed ducks who'd fuck up their quack. Tonetta must of picked the gook up from the tape we saw last night, *Platoon*, Tonetta pushing me to start Physical Confrontation, so I'll lose my privilege level. I'm cool though, smile at her, while I flip Mario mushrooms out of the top of my head. They arc through the air, smack Tonetta, she puffs to nothing with a blip. On I float, to the next obstacle. Which is, Tonetta smiles back at me, rubs and pats her rounded tummy with lovely tenderness. Bam. King Koopa zaps Mario, all five lives blink out. Tonetta came into the program too late for an abortion and now she rubs her big black ripe melon belly in my face every chance she gets, whenever she can't get at me with words or hands. Every chance, all the time, knowing the counselors were giving me BC pills, standing over me and watching me swallow, knowing if they didn't I would swell, put another mutant out in the world.

"Ladies," Louise the counselor says, "Behave. No verbal abuse."

"K-K started it," Tonetta says.

"That's Kiet, please." Louise says.

"Shee-it, whatever," Tonetta says and the other girls laugh. I am pissed at Louise for bringing it up. My name. I was Keisha when I came to Ruth's House from Crownsville Detention, but Larry got hold of my exotic I-land papers and he found Kiet, drew that name up out of the muck at the bottom of the sea, this old bone-memory he wanted me to wrap my new skin around. I had to explain to him that name was all drowned, all shriveled up and fish nibbling its eye sockets, so I tried being reasonable and said go with K-K, but he tells me no, you need to be proud of your heritage. Meaning the gook part I didn't know fuck-all about, this from Larry, he's black but he's a vet, which is like this other color, something between black and puke green. Anyway in my head I was and still am K-K. Half-a-dink, half-a-splib, my third foster dad used to call me, both his way of saying nigger.

But meanwhile the bana-gana bonana name game further pisses Tonetta off, Tonetta getting her name from the cat in the first or second whatever foster home had tried to keep her. The way she had left that place, Tonetta the kid had hung Tonetta the cat with a lamp cord to which I can relate, but still it wasn't the cat's idea. Animals get fucked over. Like, my last ex-foster father I'd run away from, in Florida? he let me go to Sea World once and I'd smoked some dope before I went and then watched the Flipper Show. Flipper this dolphin who did all of these kissy-ass doggy-type tricks for these people in wet suits that were suppose to be its TV family, though I never saw the sitcom, it was suppose to be famous. I watched and I started to identify and cry from the reefer opening me up to things, lighting up things it touched like a pinball game. Like what do you think that dolphin's real name was? Something like Glub-Click. Or Fuk Luck. Or Kiet. Swimming around. Thinking to itself: what's this Flipper shit?

"Come on, ladies," Larry says. "We'll be late for the Historical Reenactment."

We shuffle towards the tents and an open field. Prisoners in raggy gray and guards, most of them black, with muskets, walk around like fools. Inside one tent they pretending to cut off people's arms and legs, white guys in blood-stained aprons, cutting them up so they'll fit into the scene: the daffies going gag and barf. We pass an old black mama wearing a white hood and an apron; she's sitting in front of a kind of small barrel, stirring a stick in it in hard circles. I stop to look, but really to let Larry get in front of me cause Larry's stare is on my skin like dirty spiderwebs, this scared kind of sideway interest in me he got, like always looking at me for something, booby traps, I don't know what.

Stir, stir, stir. Like last night, we were watching the *Platoon* tape and I have never been able to take this scene where the bad sergeant Tom Berenger blows away this mother and threatens to kill her kid. The other daffies going burn or giggling, they're so bone ignorant, while I'm wondering if this was some history they sucked out of my memory, wondering if that was how someone did my real mom. On the screen all the GI's fighting with each other whether they should waste all the gooks or not and I don't know which side my real dad would have been on, some of the splib soldiers in the movie were on Berenger's side, some on the good sergeant's side, and I was Charlie Sheen, split in half, I could feel them all inside of me. Stir, stir, stir. Willem Dafoe, he played the good sergeant.

So I got out of the room and sat on the couch in the office upstairs, in the dark. And sure enough, Larry came up after me. He went to switch on the light. Leave it off, I told him.

"Bad movie," he said, sitting down next to me, big and heavy and kind of leaning into me, not in any kind of coming on way, but like he was really trying to see me, in the dark, moonlight coming in the window, splitting my face, Keisha blacked out, only the tipped up Kiet eyes showing, like the eyes of his enemy. Or maybe some woman he remembered, some lover he left swollen with a half-a-dink half-a-splib mutant to come swimming after him one day. When I'd run away from Florida to DC I ran to the Wall I'd seen on TV. The Wall took the high yellow out of my face and gave it back to me black, black with the white names scrawled all over it. I had walked along it slowly, letting the names write themselves across my skin, if my daddy's name was there it would have stayed on my skin when I turned from it.

"Who cares?" I said.

14

Larry shifted his weight, a creaking black heaviness next to me, the sounds of the movie drifting to us in the dark like a Historical Reenactment, screams and explosions and voices from this place where we first become some kind of garbage under each other's life.

"Don't mean nothin'," he'd said, a saying from the war, and I remembered Historic Maryland, how he and Louise had herded the daffies into a little room that said Sensurround Theatre over its door. The inside walls covered with pictures like inside the old time Founders' Ship. We all sat on benches. The doors shut. The lights went out. A voice started whispering, trickling into my brain like Larry's whisper. The movie played on all the walls around me. Creaking ropes. Waves. A voice said: "Hardship and starvation." I saw flickering people packed into the thin space of a wooden boat, heard their screams and moans, smelled their sour puke, piss, the stink of *nuoc mam* fish sauce. Sensurround. "The New World," the voice said. The lights flashed on. The movie was over.

Now a park ranger in a Smokey the Bear hat stands in front of us, megaphone in one hand, little cassette recorder in the other. Starts talking about how here on this ground under our feet blah-blah one of the largest prisoner of war camps from the Civil War, thirty thousand Confederate prisoners here, exposed to weather and abuse in Maryland. Talks about payback. While he's going on, this ragged ass white prisoner runs away and the sharp black guard I saw before raises his musket, shoots him down. Right. Just like real life. Only the prisoner too raggedy to look white. Smeared and gray. A dink. Other place, three soldier guards, black and white, pretend to beat on another prisoner. Smokey the Bear talks about how if you leave out recorders here at night, no one at all around, they pick up these ghost voices he's going to let us listen to. He turns on the recorder. Garble, garble, the voices say.

"They really get into it," I hear Louise whisper to Larry.

"And vice versa," he says.

We walk over to some white tents set up in a row, little fires and pyramids of three old time guns leaning against each other in front of each tent. "Muskets," Louise says, explaining the new world. People are taking pictures of other people, some in the tents. A man is stuffing a little boy into the mouth of the old cannon. The kid's mother is taking pictures.

"Look terrified, Jason," she says. "Stop grinning like a dork."

A group of Union soldiers march by us, led by this roostery old white man. The volunteers all black and white and waddley, fat bellies pushing out their uniforms, fat old men daffies led by a rooster. Too old to be soldiers. Or like soldiers kept forever in the army for a forever war.

Somebody beats a drum. The soldiers get into this kind of raggy line, facing me. They point their muskets at me. Run, run, run, run, run, the voices on the tape say to me. The rooster man pulls out a sword and yells readyaimfire. The flash and the noise split me in half. Blow Kiet away from Keisha. Dink from splib.

I look back at the soldiers. They load and fire again. If I worked here I'd play a VC, I'd squat down near the entrance to a reconstructed straw hootch, rocking my baby, waiting while the tourists, dressed as GI's, came into the village. Then I'd rise up, reveal the weapon hidden under my baby and pretend to blow them away. Then one day I'd forget where I really was. I'd put real bullets in the gun. I'd have a flashback and shoot a tourist, thinking he was a GI, come to rape and murder. Then, before anyone realized what happened, I'd run. I'd hide in the marshes. I'd be the last VC.

"Fire!" the rooster says.

The soldiers load and fire again.

"Fix bayonets," the rooster says.

The soldiers stick their bayonets on the end of their muskets. They point them at me and charge, yelling, their faces twisted.

I back up a little bit from the faces and stumble into Tonetta. She cusses me under her breath and pushes me into the stacked muskets. They fall with a clatter. The soldiers stop a few feet from me and threaten with their bayonets. I pick up one of the fallen muskets.

"Look terrified, bitch," I say to Tonetta.

"Kiet, put it down," Larry says. He steps in front of me. I see myself reflected in his shades, black-clad, holding a weapon.

"We're here now," I tell him. I point the gun at him.

He looks at me and backs up, funny smile on his face.

"Don't mean nothin,'" I tell him.

"For your own safety," the announcer on the PA says, "please do not handle the weapons."

The musket is heavier than I thought it would be. I wonder what will happen. Everybody is looking at me. You can't trust the gooks, I'd say. Then I'd pull the trigger. The flash would leap out and hit Larry's chest. Maybe he'd have a heart attack and die, his last sight: my face. Or maybe he'd jump at me. I'd club his hands and turn and run.

Even as I think this, I club down at his hands and I'm turning and then I am running, a part of me still running in my head, but my feet really pounding against the grass. I zig-zag in the direction of the parking lot, holding onto the musket. Behind me, I hear Louise and Larry calling K-K as if to please me, but I keep on running: what's this Flipper shit? If I look over my shoulder now, I know I'll see the two of them and the guards and the prisoners, all chasing me, muskets in their hands, their faces red and angry. I know I'll see armies of mad old men, all dressed like soldiers, all chasing after me.

NESTING

"HIRAM JOHNS SHOULD BE fragged," Tom Vessey said.

Brian turned and stared at him. He felt a flash of rage.

Louise Hallam had just told them about one of her charges, a Vietnamese girl, who had run away from the group home where she'd been brought after she had been molested by Johns during the time she was fostered to him and his wife. Heloise Johns had died, of liver cancer, six months before, and the girl should have been removed much sooner, though apparently she wasn't the first of the Johns' foster children to be molested. Vessey had become incensed at the story. But Brian found himself irrationally angry now at the man's use of the term "fragged," as if Vessey had usurped something, ripped off an artifact from Brian's past. Vessey was working on a smart bomb project called Whisper Shadow for the Naval Air Weapons Test Center. Worked in the war business, but spent the war the word fragged came from as he would the coming one, designing weapons systems, sending them away from himself to do their damage and be destroyed, as if they were the soldiers who had gone in his place.

Brian realized he was enjoying his righteous anger. It irritated him even more.

"Can I get you a drink, Tom?" Mary asked.

"I'm sorry," he said. "I thought I was past the capacity to be shocked."

21

"It does shock," Mary said. "It's sick and perverse and tawdry, right here in River City."

Tom and Mary both swiveled, as if drawn, to look at the circle of children dancing around the bonfire. The light from the fire flickered against the tree trunks on the lawn, strobed the picnic table laden with corn, steamed crabs, ribs, chicken. Brian tried to let the sight soothe his strange mood.

The Halloween party was a tradition he had initiated two years before. At first he'd tried to get everyone to dress up as figures from local history: their small neighborhood was on the northern border of the Point Lookout state park, and he was working the Civil War prison camp site at Point Lookout, engaged—with what he'd once heard Russell Hallam describe as "Jewish urgency"—in digging up the bones of some of the thousands of prisoners killed there. Brian had been unmoved by the ethnic slur, if that's what it was: he sensed a deeper resentment in Russell's remark. Maybe he felt usurped.

"What really infuriates me," Mary said, "is that he'll get away with it."

Alex Hallam, the county sheriff, sipped at a plastic cup of cider. "Johns was arrested and charged," he said slowly. "But if we can't locate the girl, the case will be dropped. That's how it works."

"And he's a SMIB from an old family and that's how it works," Louise said bitterly, Southern Maryland Inbred: it was an acronym Brian had never heard Louise let pass her lips before. "Mary's right, they won't touch him. Even if she testifies, most we'd see is Mr. Johns picking up litter along Route Five for a week, some community service dealie. He'll probably just use the trash he gets for nesting."

"There's no proof he does that," Alex said firmly, as if Louise had stepped beyond the bounds by mentioning that crime. As if nesting, Brian thought, the putting of foreign objects, trash, into bundles of tobacco going to auction to increase their weight, might be perceived as worse than child molestation, here, among the SMIB's.

"That child came to us with vaginal infections," Louise said vehemently, "though apparently there was no penile penetration. You ever see Johns' fingers? You ever see his nails? That nesting son of a bitch."

"Louise," Alex Hallam said.

His wife was holding a paper plate heaped with beans, corn bread and chicken. The bottom sagged and dripped: none of the food had been touched.

"The sexually-challenged Farmer Johns," Russell Hallam said, smiling unpleasantly at Brian.

He was dressed in a complete Union soldier's uniform, the only costumed adult there, the only black person; his choice of dress, Brian understood, was to be considered ironic, a pointed jibe at him. The deputy was a local history buff and at first had been pleased that Brian wanted to hear his family stories. But he had grown increasingly irked at the focus in Brian's research on the atrocities committed by the black regiment at Point Lookout, old fraggings scattered under the marshy tip of the state: Russell supposedly was a descendent of one of the Union guards at the camp.

"Any news on the whereabouts of the girl?" he asked.

"The whereabouts?" Russell's lips twitched slightly, as if he'd tasted something bad. "Don't you know," he said, "she owns the night."

Brian looked away from him, towards the children. Terminators, Ninja Turtles, and now a few Desert Shield Warriors in tan and white fatigues had popped up among the more traditional witches and ghosts. Some of the kids had sparklers. They ran in the darkness of the meadow, spinning them in wide circles and throwing them into the air. The sparklers streaked across the darkness like tracers in a firefight.

Turning, Brian saw a look cross Russell's and Alex's faces, as if their nerves were wired together. At that instant he was sure the three of them had made the same visual connection, the ghosts of the coming war dancing into the ghosts of their war.

The other deputy, Trung, smiled. "We'll probably get the kid on a B&E," he said. "You know how to tell a Vietnamese-American's burglarized your house? Your dog is gone and your math homework's been done."

"Stop trying so hard," Russell told him.

"I really want to kill him," Louise said softly. "With my own hands. I didn't know I had it in me." She was trembling. Alex put an arm around her shoulder, but she shrugged it off.

"He should be fragged," Vessey said again.

It's not your word, Brian thought. You can't have it.

"Traditionally," he said, "an individual like Johns, his behavior, would be seen as too big a threat to the social fabric to have him around. The tribe would cut him out. Take him out."

Russell grinned at him. "Top him like a tobacco plant, right? Johns go with the territory, don't he doc—you think so? Something twisty under the grace of the country, come nest up into you, crud up your lung lace. Something maybe best left buried."

The grace of the country, Brian thought.

But said: "You ever notice how you change your grammatical patterns, Russell, whenever you bait me?"

Russell's grin widened. "Old tradition."

"Old tradition," Louise nodded. "Here's one—my dad would have taken Hiram Johns out on the boat, dropped him off, trot-lined with him. Vessey's right," she said. "We should frag the bastard. Cut off his balls for crab bait. That's what my dad would have done."

All of the men at the party stirred and said nothing and didn't meet each others' eyes.

Brian didn't really believe that the soil of a place could be stained by the curses of its history, though he could understand how elegant and deadly hauntings could be drawn in Russell's eyes under the grace of the country: veined and lovely spreads of broad leaf that called no connection to the eye with the black crud caked in the membrane lace of lungs, neat launchpad rows of tobacco plants echoing in form and function the clean beautiful lines of the weapons designed and tested at the naval air base. Whisper shadows nested everywhere under the green pretty landscape.

Things came around, he supposed, but he still felt an archaeologist's distrust of the symmetry of the occasion when his Israeli cousin showed up at his house on the day after Halloween. He had gone to live for a time in Israel just after he'd come back from the war; while he was there he had come to think of himself by his Hebrew name. Now, twenty years later, the child of the relatives with whom he'd stayed—a boy just out of the army himself—had just come to his Maryland door and introduced himself by the same name, as if Brian's own younger self had dropped in for a visit.

"My Hebrew name is Yossi also," he said to his son.

"Yossi and Yossi. Boy that's dumb," Zeke said.

The echo of the names caught in Brian's mind.

"What kind of name is 'Zeke'?" his cousin asked, drawing out the word. He watched Yossi reach over and rough Zeke's hair. "An American name," Zeke said, grinning. Brian felt a little relieved. The boy, eight years old, usually adopted a teasing, sarcastic manner towards relatives who would overly praise his cuteness or smartness, exaggerate their pleasure at being in his presence. His attitude sometimes pleased him, as if his son was an imp—a secret name—he could free from his heart to say the things he no longer dared or could afford to say. Sometimes. But now he was afraid Yossi would just see a spoiled American brat.

"Why's my dad need an Israeli name anyway?"

Yossi shrugged.

Zeke peered at him doubtfully. "Do you know how to play Metroid?"

"Sure."

"You know how?"

"Yes, of course."

"Zeke, Yossi just got here," Brian said, "We've hardly had a chance to talk."

25

"You mean Yossi wants to talk to Yossi," Zeke teased.

"I don't mind," Yossi said, something in his voice reminding Brian of the relief it had been to play with the kids when he'd come to stay with Yossi's parents, a break from their kind but relentless interrogation about his own parents, his service in the American military.

"Go ahead," he said. "But just for a few minutes, Zeke."

Zeke led Yossi to his room. In a minute, Brian heard the electronic bleeping of the game. In the paper a few days before, he'd read about an American immigrant to Israel who'd introduced a video game based on the intifada: you blipped little running Palestinians. He put up some coffee and sat down on the couch, listening to Zeke's excited voice. *What's your name, cousin?* Yossi's father Danny had asked, when he'd arrived at his cousin's house on the moshav.

Brian.

No, b'ivrit, *in Hebrew. Not your American name. Your Jewish name.*

Yosef. After my grandfather, Brian had said. Yosef was the root from which his maternal family, in America and Israel, branched—his parents had been immigrants, DP's who had met in a camp in Germany: Brian, his American name, he suspected, had been given both as a hope and as camouflage.

Twenty years ago, Danny had grinned and kissed his son's stomach. Like this one, he'd said. Yossi and Yossi. Then he winked, encompassing Brian into a mutual history. The Yosef both Yossi and he were named after was a pious Jew who had had to kill a Polish deserter who was threatening his family. Yosef had hit the man with a frozen branch, but the act of violence, according to Brian's mother, was so abhorrent to his nature that his own body punished him shortly afterwards with a stroke, the arm he had used to wield the branch going dead, frozen. Brian's parents had both fled massacre and burning villages, fled people who regarded them as subhuman and killed casually, and when, in the war, he heard men speak of the Vietnamese as animal-like, dirty, indifferent to death and easy to kill, he'd stood back

26

from them inside his parents', Yosef's, understanding. He couldn't even bring himself to use the word gook. Of course his moral finickiness didn't last; it wasn't the kind of war where it could, and when he had finally pressed himself close enough to it and allowed himself to hate as well as kill, he'd felt nothing more than a kind of relief, the elation of a cossack.

As if the thought were an invocation, Danny's son, Yosef's other namesake, came back into Brian's living room now and sat silently on his couch, burly as his father, but his hair black and cropped short, coarser, his eyebrows heavier, eyes lidded and duller, movements slower: he had Danny's strength, but his father's air of shamed, intelligent ambiguity about that strength was missing, as if strained at last from this generation.

Mary entered, and Yossi held out his hand awkwardly. She shook it and smiled politely and asked about his trip. Brian was suddenly aware of the smell of stale sweat, an acrid foreignness intruding into the small room. He could see a faint twitch of distress, a tightness in his wife's face that he found he resented; Yossi had been on the road, what did she expect?

"Would you like to take a shower before dinner?" she asked.

"That's all right," Yossi said.

They were snagged in a silence. Brian looked at his wife, reading her annoyance at this intrusion, her Lutheran wariness: Yossi, darkly hirsute, thick set, standing in his comfortable, utterly self-possessed Israeli silence, was the child of a choice Brian had almost made.

"You just got out of the army?" he said in Hebrew.

"Yes?" Yossi said, his response a surprised question, an Israeli way that brought Brian back again.

"When I first went to Israel," he said, "I was about your age. Just out of the army, like you, and I wanted to travel, not be tied down. It was just after the war."

"Yes, my father told me."

"You were just a baby. But now you've been a soldier too."

Yossi let another silence gather between them.

"Blech, blech, blech," Zeke said, imitating the gutturals of the Hebrew. He'd come in after Yossi.

"Did you go to Europe?" Brian asked.

Yossi looked questioningly at him, and he realized he'd asked the question in English.

"A little. But I wanted to come here. For Israelis, we like to come to the United States." He waved helplessly. "The movies."

"Has it been like the movies?"

"You know, only this place." Yossi's smile was a surprise; it made his face look animated and intelligent. "Little houses, fields, the river. Like the United States of the movies."

Brian looked out of the window. Sparrows were landing on the lawn, spilling in an arc from the sky. They kept coming, as if they were being poured, scattering over an acre of ground, pecking, feeding. He saw a rabbit dart across the lawn and into the tangled jungle of ivy and wild roses that grew between the screen of locust trees along the road. Their leaves moved in a breeze that came in a second to his skin, the land that would go into his name spreading flat and to the trees, an empty, close-cut space on which he could easily spot movement, the flicker of a rabbit, the approach of an enemy.

"This area always reminded me of the Jezreel. Or the Bet Shean, near your moshav."

Yossi snorted. "No, I don't think so."

"What are you doing today, Dad?" Zeke asked.

"I may take Yossi out to the dig. Want to come?"

"Nope."

"Why not?"

Zeke shrugged. "Are you going to get me a tape?"

"You have to do more this weekend than watch tapes and play Nintendo. Are you reading anything?"

"*The Lion, The Witch and the Wardrobe.*"

"Again?"

"I like it."

Zeke looked at him. "Pick me up, Dad."

"You're too big."

28

"Pick me up."

He took his son under the armpits and held him up, Zeke's arms going around his neck, legs wrapping around his waist, the warm weight of him. He wondered how long he'd have this. He thought of Johns and shuddered, wondered what the farmer's need sought in a child's embrace. When Mary would be on night duty at the hospital and they were alone in the house, Zeke would crawl into bed and snuggle into his back and he'd read to him from the *Chronicles of Narnia* about how human children, the sons of Adam and the daughters of Eve, went through the darkness in the back of the closet into a bright kingdom where they battled evil, a place where evil and time and death could be defeated. He pressed Zeke to himself and kissed the top of his head.

"Mushers," Zeke said.

"Tell Yossi you want to be excused."

"I thought you were Yossi."

"So go tell Yossi that Yossi told you to say you want to be excused."

"You're not funny, Dad."

"So do you want to go to the dig with us."

"No."

"Why not?"

"It's boring. Were you and Yossi's dad in the war together?"

"A war happened when I was in Israel, but I wasn't in it. Do you know the difference between Israel and Vietnam?"

He saw Zeke flinch and heard the edge in his voice. Zeke said, "You won't let me see *Platoon* or rent the game. Woody's dad lets him get it."

"Is your name Woody? Anyway, what's that have to do with it?"

"Was Yossi in the army?"

Yossi and Brian caught each other's eye, then looked away, to the blank television screen, as if seeing what connected them on it, flowing to join under the glass of the set. Yossi got up suddenly, squatted in front of the set and pulled the on switch.

The sudden light flickered into a commercial, then the news theme. Brian feared what pictures would appear next, flare out of their minds onto the screen: soldiers with clubs, rock-throwing children; there had been coverage of the Palestinian uprising almost every night that week, along with news of the Gulf buildup. He tried to picture his cousin, the Jewish cossack finally reconstructed, his face masked by a plastic visor, his arm swinging in wild arcs against dark, scattering forms.

Yossi reached over and switched off the television, as if he had shared Brian's fear.

"Where were you?" Brian asked. "In the army?"

"Somewhere in Israel." Yossi grinned at his use of the stock phrase, the smile again emerging like a hidden person under the sheened blankness of the visor.

"And in the territories?" Brian insisted. "The intifada?"

"It's a complicated situation," Yossi said.

Brian snorted. Yossi looked down, a student who had given the wrong answer.

"Maybe not so complicated," Brian said, then felt disgusted with himself at baiting this boy—he hadn't the right, hadn't chosen to live in Israel, be Yossi; he'd become Brian, bunkered in here in the United States of the movies.

"You were in the Israeli army, huh?" Zeke said. "Wow, like I'm really impressed."

Brian gave Zeke a look. His son made a face; Brian's own expression exaggerated in miniature. Yossi reached over and rumpled the boy's hair. Brian felt a twinge of panic—Yossi's large, capable hand, a soldier's hand, moving towards the boy—that surprised and shamed him.

Yossi was still looking at the ground. Startled, Brian saw that his Israeli cousin's eyes had brimmed with tears.

He decided not to go to the dig. Instead he showed his cousin the boat he was trying to get into shape, a fourteen foot oak and cedar Old Town, trimmed with Philippine mahogany. He'd spotted it rotting outside a barn in Chopticon and paid the farmer who owned it fifty dollars. He had it up on a trailer next to the shed now. The two of them were standing and looking at it, when Alex Hallam pulled up. His appearance startled Brian. Not the fact he'd stopped by, but how tired he looked. He was in uniform and presumably on duty, but unshaven, disheveled.

He grinned at the boat. "You going to get yourself out on the water, Brian?"

"Part of my assimilation campaign: Jordy Hewitt"—he named a waterman who lived nearby—"calls me 'that digging and drawing and writing fella.' He grins and shakes his head when he says it, as if he can't figure how I get by like that, not doing any real work."

Alex smiled and nodded at Yossi.

Brian introduced him.

"Where you from, Hossi," Alex said, shaking his hand.

"Israel."

"Yossi just got out of the army. He's a farmer," Brian felt compelled to tell Alex, as if to say we're not all drawing and writing and accounting and lawyering fellas.

Alex grunted, as if withholding judgment.

Brian patted the boat. "I want to sand the bottom, caulk it, paint it. But first we need to get it off the trailer and upside down."

Yossi went into the shed. In a minute he came out, carrying two small saw horses, then two more. He went back in and came out with several two-by-fours, the tool set. Brian watched Alex watching Yossi. His cousin quickly and efficiently lined up and nailed a board between two saw horses. Brian fixed up the other set and put them next to the boat, while Alex rummaged around, came out with the varnish, caulk and anti-fouling paint.

"Heavy boat," he said to Yossi.

Yossi did his shrug. He fingered the metal rope loop at the bow, walked to the stern, touched the loops there.

"Do you have two long *ahmodim*. How do you say, sticks?"

"There's some old poles behind the shed."

Yossi got them, then tapped the loops. He pantomimed levering the boat over.

They slid the poles through. Brian got ready to turn the boat, but he saw Alex looking oddly at Yossi, who was staring thoughtfully at the boat. He wondered what both of them saw—he felt outside of whatever was passing between them. Yossi walked over to the hinged, glassless windshield and pulled it out. He swung it back and forth in its arc. A slight grin fluttered on Alex's lips. Yossi took the coil of rubberized clothesline Brian had in the tool box and lashed the windshield to its frame. When they turned the boat over, Brian saw now, the windshield would have swung out and hit the ground. He saw Alex catch Yossi's eye and nod at him as if he'd passed a test Brian hadn't even known was going on.

"What's up?" he asked. There was something official in Alex's demeanor. Though it wasn't unusual for him to drop over. When they'd first met, Alex, in a friendly, welcome neighbor conversation, had put Brian through a subtle and efficient interrogation about his background, finding out, among other things that they'd both been in the war the same year, both helicopter crew, though in different branches of service. It had been his day to pass some sort of Alex Hallam test, though they never talked about the war again. Alex, caught up in the sudden rush of revelations they'd both been surprised into, volunteered that he had been crew in one of the helicopters that had inserted Charlie Company into My Lai 4, released murder onto that village. The confession pushed Brian into silence and neither that day nor since could he bring himself to speak to Alex about it, ask what he'd seen, what he'd done. Brian hadn't been there, hadn't seen anything like it in the war, yet My Lai had somehow stained into his memories to become something he owned as well. Yosef's eyes behind his own taking in the photos of grinning GI's, carrying weapons he'd once carried, standing over the heaped dead in a ditch in the red laterite mud of Quang Ngai that led back in time to other grinning soldiers with machine guns standing over the ditches his parents had barely escaped.

"I'm still looking for that girl," Alex said. "Wanted to know if you'd seen anything unusual."

"No." Brian laughed. "No more unusual than usual anyway. Mary made a find," he said to Alex's look. "By accident, with the dog. Complete, but with both hands missing, saw marks on the wrist bones, the kind of crude amputation they did at the prison hospital."

"I ought to come have a look." It was standard procedure to have someone from the sheriff's department notified when new remains were found, though Brian felt that Alex and Russell, white and black Hallams, were more interested in the finds themselves, their bones marrowed into this ground.

"Why don't you bring Russell?" he said. "I think he knows about it already. I think it agitates him."

"It's his hide you're digging into. Take him seriously."

"I was just thinking about that. Seeing it like that. And seriously is the only way I ever take Russell."

"I hear you might be going back to Vietnam, dig there," Alex said, casually, apropos of nothing, of everything.

Brian nodded. He'd received an invitation to join an anthropological forensic team excavating the remains of American MIA's. He felt a cold heavy bar of dread slide into his stomach, at the connection Alex's words flicked into him of scraping into his own flesh and body and skull.

"Any idea where the girl might be?" he asked.

"She's out there someplace." Alex hesitated, grinned. He rested his hand on the boat, rubbed his palm over the wood. "I was going to say, 'like a disturbance.' I have no idea why."

"I feel like she's dug into my hide too. Remember what Tom Vessey said at the party? He's right. I hope someone will frag Johns."

"Tom Vessey's a pogue," Alex said. "And you don't need to be saying things like that."

"Not to the county sheriff?"

33

"I know who you are, Brian. I'm not Jordy Hewitt, or Russell either—you don't need to impress me."

Brian looked at him, a big man with a dark Indian shock of hair, saturnine face, full, sensual Southern lips that usually seemed quivering with the same hidden amusement Brian sometimes felt in his own heart, something from the part of his own history that coffled him to Alex, to Russell: Hallam and Hallam and Yossi and Yossi and the runaway girl; they knew what could swing loose, cause breakage, consequences. But Alex's lips were compressed now, the sheriff's face so intent it seemed pulled tight to its bones. He had heard stories that when Alex was young he'd had a talent for sculpture. Rural Delights, Mary had said, when he told her Hallam had won an art scholarship at one time: she regarded such anecdotes as tactics to make her feel she was living in a place whose seeming narrowness concealed unexpected and charming eccentricities. But it was not the surprise of that shaping talent, but rather the knowledge of its loss, the will to be damaged, that drew him to Alex Hallam.

"Is this something you'd do yourself usually?" he asked. "Look for a missing kid?"

Alex stared at him, his eyes tired, pouched under with dark bags.

"Who else?" he said.

Brian began his run late in the afternoon: a mile down Wheeler Road to where it ended just before the river. The top half of the road was paved; the bottom, along Johns' twenty acres, was packed dirt, embedded with exposed vertebrae-nubs of whitened oyster shells. Stopping, standing on the road, he could see the swing set the old man had built between his white clapboard house and the silver-boarded curing barn, its hinged slats winged out from the bottom.

He heard the chains on the swings clanging against the metal poles, coming to him across five acres of tobacco field. The swing set was bright as a lure in the clear air. The field was stubbled with lines marking the harvested tobacco plants. Forest bordered the other two sides of the field; at the end of the road was a tree-lined bank past which the land opened into an expanse of water.

A German shepherd, caged in a cyclone fence enclosure, was leaping frantically at the wire, barking at him. The carping noise opened up his anger. A man, Johns, came out of the house, his breath steaming. He kicked at the cage, then looked over at Brian, cupped his hands and shouted something; Brian thought he heard the word *move*, or *love*, or *Jew*. Johns' face seemed distorted, angry, even at this distance. Brian jogged on.

He was nearly at the end of the dirt road. Road's end, land's end, the water beyond. The tall sentries of loblolly pine marking the division. Usually at this point he would turn and start home. He should go; he'd left Yossi alone with Mary and Zeke. He hesitated, looking down at the white ribbon of sand, oyster shell and fossil beach stretching off to the right.

He jumped down onto it. Some exposed roots blocked the beach; he waded around them into the cold grip of the water, then came back onto the sand and started to run again. After a few hundred yards he could see a fringe of dark water fingering off the creek, an inlet that ended in a crotch of cord grass, glistening with spider webs. A blue heron, startled by his presence, lifted beautifully and silently into the air. He could see the tangled forest that held both banks, dark crooked branches hanging out over the water; on the left bank these woods would extend all the way down to Point Lookout. He entered them. Unseen, unheard. Whisper-Shadow coming into the kingdom of Whisper-Shadow. A copperhead rippled out like a released boobytrap from under a small teepee of dead branches; a spider web brushed his face like the teasing touch of trip wires. He went deeper into it, until he could see the other side of the house and the silver-boarded barn and the yellow-stubbled fields and the caged dog, and then, startlingly, Johns himself, unaware that he was being watched, pushing the swings. The farmer's face was empty of expression. Brian watched him move into the barn.

The trees soughed and scraped around him. He lay very still. It was dark now. The hinged boards in the barn were alternatively winged open from the bottom. He could glimpse the rafters where spears of tobacco hung to be air-cured. Music from a country station blasted into the night, across the space between himself and the barn. Light leaked through the open slats and lay in yellow bars on the ground. Everything was clear and exaggerated. "I'm looking for a better way," the music wailed. He moved his eyes to the dog cage. It looked dark and empty. He kept focused on it until he could make out the bulk of the dog, like a thickening of the darkness, in the corner. It was licking itself, whimpering, as if Johns had beat it. Then it rose, its teeth gleaming, as if it had felt Brian's gaze. It lunged at the wire, barking. He froze. No one came out of the barn. Maybe the music was too loud.

The air was cold on his skin, no dream. He came out from the trees, staying between the yellow stripes of light painted on the ground. He drew close, closer. He was near enough now to peer through the opening beneath the angle of a slat. The rich dry smell of tobacco leaves pushed back out at him. A boot, its heel steel-capped, came down almost in front of his face, just beyond the opening. Another joined it. He was close enough to see the scuffing on the leather. The boots walked away. Jeans, a blue-checkered shirt, the back of Johns' head grew in the narrow space between the boards. Johns began placing the cured tobacco leaves into wicker bundling forms. He was thin but had heavy, corded forearms: Brian was close enough to see Johns' muscles move under his sweaty, dusty skin as he worked, his hands, the probing spatulate fingers, the broken nails black and filthy, packing a weight of filth and trash into the delicate center of the plants. Nesting. A wave of revulsion washed through Brian, the emotion so precise and clean that he continued to stare at Johns' hands, hoping the sight would stir it out again. The tissues of his own hands were tingling with something like thirst. The air was thick with the dust-dry acrid sweetness of the leaves; it smelled like insanity. He felt the blood shiver in his arms and chest. The shiver moved onto his skin, up his neck and scalp, into his fingers. He knew if he didn't leave now, get out at once, he would never get home again.

Mary trailed her hand down his chest. "There weren't any tears. You just saw yourself, your own compassion."

"Is that what it was?"

"Why is it so important to you that I like him?"

There was a business card on the night table, propped against the base of the lamp. Brian picked it up and looked at it.

"How long will he stay?" Mary asked.

"I'm not sure."

"Why don't you just come out and ask him?"

"Asking him when he's leaving is like asking him to leave."

"My God, Brian."

"The funny thing is, if I were Israeli, I probably wouldn't think twice about asking, being that blunt," he said. "But still, I lived for months with his parents; I was never asked that question." Then he said, to her look: "Oh, I don't mean he'll be here for months."

He turned the card between his fingers. "Did the broker call today?"

"No, not yet. It's part of the whole ceremony. The twisting in the wind. To be sure we're worthy."

He looked at the card. On one side was a list of names. If he had questions, he was to talk to Julie for inquiries about scheduling and costs, Kristen for disbursements, Susan for escrow releases, Tuyet for payments. For what things cost. The Sisters of Our Lady of Equity. Tuyet. The one Vietnamese name stood out, encompassed yet here, in his Maryland bedroom.

"When are we worthy?" he asked.

"You're never sure. That's part of the ceremony too." She took the card from him and looked at the names. "You know what he's saying here? Don't bother me, I have women to handle the shit work. You notice he never talks to me when we're in the office. It's like you're applying for a mortgage for yourself."

Lately Brian had been waking up in the middle of the night, worried about getting the mortgage, putting what was around them, the bunker, into his name. A familiar panic would scramble in his chest and he'd be fully awake, sweating, as if he had heard mortars falling outside, shaking the walls. They were renting the house with an option, but the loan officer had been very cautious—with both their incomes they made enough to qualify, but they owed too many debts: he wasn't sure they could make the payments.

"See Tuyet for payments," Brian said.

Mary moved her hand onto her belly, as if to show what had been paid.

"I'm sorry," he said.

She closed her eyes. "I dreamt it was a girl," she said. "I dreamt I saw her face at our window. Out in the dark."

He knew Mary was speaking about her miscarriage, but for some reason, the word "girl," he supposed, or the name Tuyet, he thought again of the Vietnamese girl, the foster child Johns had abused. He felt the same twist of fear and cold rage in his chest that he'd felt when he saw Johns in his barn: he'd wanted to erase the perverted bastard, blot him from the same world where Zeke lived. He didn't say anything to Mary now. She'd lost the child shortly after the incident with Johns was reported and she hated to talk about the molestations.

"It wasn't a girl," he said. "It wasn't anything yet."

"It was. She was." Mary took his hand, pressed it against her stomach. Against the absence. "She was, she would have been. I know. I carried her. That's where the term comes from."

"Maybe it's because I didn't feel it, her, in me," he said. "When you were pregnant with Zeke, he was nothing to me. An abstraction. But then an hour after he was born, I knew I'd die for him, die protecting him. I'd certainly kill for him. Yet before he was here, I couldn't imagine feeling like that."

38

She ran a finger over his cheek, to his lips.

"What a strange way to put it. I don't think of dying for Zeke —the opposite. I mean, I would, I'd 'die for him,'" she said the phrase as if it were in quotation marks, "But I don't think of it that way."

"Would you kill for him?"

She looked at him oddly. He heard a noise, an alien shuffle, in the hall.

"At least there's someone here for Zeke," he said.

"What a funny thing to say, Brian." She turned over on her side, away from him.

He put his arms around her waist, socketed himself up against her. She pushed her hips back into him. He rolled her flannel nightgown up to her waist, feeling himself flop hard against the cleft of her behind. She reached around, gripped his penis, then withdrew her hand, with a small, exasperated laugh, as if at the existence of a desire that outlived its issue. "Your timing is shitty," she said. Her muscles were rigid; she'd been squeezing out, recoiling, he realized, not pushing into him.

"Look, I'm sorry," she said. "I'm just grumpy."

He kissed the back of her neck, reached over and turned off the light. "It's OK."

In fact it was. He realized he was relieved; the need he'd felt wasn't for sex. In a while he heard her breathing deepen. He stared at the ceiling, feeling the desire drain from him. With its absence, fear returned, a hollow bubble expanding in his chest. He remembered what Louise Hallam had told him about her troubled girl; she was half-Vietnamese, her father probably a black GI. Before going to Johns, the kid had run away from other foster homes, had lived on the street, on drugs; she had a confused self-image, Louise had said, and laughed self-consciously at the terminology. He didn't think they were called troubled girls anymore either. See Tuyet for payments. In the dark now, in his sleepy brain, Louise's Vietnamese girl trembled into his unborn daughter, self-images confused: troubled girls, troubling girls hovering near his windows, peering in, scratching at the glass. Begging for his protection. He flowed out of the house, going back through the woods to Johns' house. Over the hills and through the woods, and not stopping this time behind the line he'd drawn for himself yesterday. Here I am. He'd probably killed or helped to kill better people in Vietnam. No, not probably. He heard the soft shuffle from the hall again and he coaxed open the front door, pushed against it with his mind, and let Yossi, a silent, helmeted golem, slip out, sent him spinning to Johns. Yossi's face, the twisted malevolent face he pictured under the rim of the helmet was, he realized, a Nazi caricature of a Jew. He lowered the plastic visor so there was no face and only the reflected face of the moon and he saw Tuyet's face, saw it again as if it was the face of his own unborn daughter, named and emerging from the green jungle as she caught sight of Yossi and Yossi, silent twins moving towards her through the trees; he saw her face fall into fright, he saw her run.

Yossi stayed around the house the next day, working in the garden the way Brian had worked his father's land twenty years before. He brought the roto-tiller Brian had given up on back to life and churned the soil in the thirty by fifty plot, furrowing vertically and then horizontally and then diagonally, crossing and crisscrossing until the soil threatened to become fine as sand and Brian had to call him in and say *maspeek*, Yossi, enough, rest, Zeke wants to play with you.

Yet he seemed to be more animated, smiling frequently, acting out the same healing metamorphoses Brian had thought to enact when he'd stayed with Yossi's parents. And Brian was glad he was around to be with Zeke. The boy was eight, an age when he saw his neighbors' kids walk or bike over on their own to each others' houses. He'd considered it a safe area before Johns' arrest, and even now he knew Zeke still had to learn to be independent. But he was worried whenever Zeke went out on his own and now if he or Mary was at work, at least he knew that Yossi would be with Zeke, playing video games, wrestling:

although he understood Mary's objection. It was like having two kids in the house again. But seeing Zeke's lit-up face, hearing his shrieks of delight as Yossi tossed him, swung him upside down, Mary, Brian felt, was warming to his cousin. Yet what if her apprehensions were right, some mother's instinct telling her something was off here? Watching Yossi sitting hunched over the kitchen table, hulking and silent and blank, Brian remembered the fantasy he'd had about him: a part of himself come back, a golem he might have set loose with the force of his hate for Johns; Yossi's hands still competent at the arcs of violence in the world, his heart emptied of restraints and compassion.

Mad vet flips out. Stop it.

He brought Yossi out with Alex and Russell Hallam to see the bones Mary had found near the dig, but his cousin was no more moved by the site than Zeke. The digs Brian had worked on in Israel when he'd first become interested in archaeology were more ancient and he supposed, to most non-archaeologists, more dramatic. Seeing what had emerged from the solid earth under their feet, Yossi remained silent, almost militantly noncommittal, as if to say this was not his ground, not his crime.

That evening Mary had an all night shift, and after she left for work, Brian fixed hot dogs and beans and sat with Yossi and Zeke in front of the television, watching cartoons. "It's a boys' night," he explained to Zeke, who seemed delighted at the idea. Brian cleared the dishes from the folding tables. When he returned from the kitchen, he saw that Yossi's face had changed, gone to the set dullness of those first days; his cousin sat slumped on the couch, his hands dangling between his knees. On the screen were the images they had tried to banish from the house: the hate-twisted faces of rock-throwing children, soldiers charging with arcing, falling clubs that they wielded like heavy branches, their arms drained finally of grandpa Yosef's weakness. He looked

41

away, inadvertently catching Yossi's eye as he did, and their gazes slid past each other, Yossi looking away from Yossi.

His cousin wiped his face. Zeke looked at him, then got up and turned off the TV. He went over to Yossi.

"Look strong."

Yossi grinned blankly. "What?"

"Look strong. You know." Zeke snapped into a muscleman pose. "Make a muscle."

Yossi made a muscle, a grin twisting his face, lighting it oddly. Zeke's finger shot towards his armpit, tickling. Yossi grabbed the boy and swung him up over his head, the swishing arc of the motion slicing at Brian's heart, Zeke's skull brushing sickeningly close to the ceiling. Yossi swung the boy upside down, Zeke's face close, too close to the floor and now Brian's Israeli cousin, laughing, grabbed his son and swung him up to his shoulder and over and down, thudding him onto the rug, Yossi's face suffused with light, and Brian was on his feet suddenly, grabbing the bunched power of Yossi's arm, the massive, sweated muscle twitching under his palm, and he yelled, "Cut it out, Yossi, enough."

The animation drained from Yossi's face, leaving a dull, passive mask with wounded eyes. He put Zeke down and shambled from the room.

Zeke stared after him, his eyes filming. "Sometimes you're such a dork, Dad," he said.

In the morning, Brian brewed coffee and tried to read the paper. Yossi was up; he could hear noises from his room. When he came out, Brian smiled at him and he smiled back weakly, but his eyes still fled, as if they shared memory and shame, and when Brian asked him if he wanted coffee, he shook his head. A moment later the sound of a motor broke the morning, and when Brian looked out of the window he saw Yossi behind the tiller, moving back and forth, trapped in the square of the garden patch.

"Dad, can we go get some crabs?" Zeke asked.

"I'm tired, Zeke."

"Dad, I think it would be a good idea," Zeke said, looking out at Yossi, and Brian looked at his son, felt blessed with undeserved luck.

The dock they used was on the eastern side of the ten acre meadow bordering the rear of their lot: the meadow ended in a wooded slope that went down to the creek, an estuary off the Potomac. The land was once part of a tobacco farm bought by the same developer who was selling the house; when more families moved in they would have sharing rights on the dock, but meanwhile the meadow and the dock were theirs and on this day, with Yossi and Zeke, he walked through the johnsongrass and Queen Anne's lace and necklaces of late blooming blue cornflowers, down to the water. Zeke walked between them, holding their hands, and they lifted him so his feet flew above the meadow. "Higher, Yossi and Yossi," he shouted. When they brought him down, walking between them fast, Yossi stuck his leg out in front of Zeke so that the boy sprawled, laughing. "Daddy, he's torturing me, he's an Israeli torturer," Zeke yelled, bounding up, and Brian tripped him also. "Yossi and Yossi," Zeke said from the ground, "suck." Brian looked at Yossi and they both grinned.

"Where'd you pick up that language, champ?"

"What language?"

Yossi grabbed Zeke under his arms, and Brian took his legs, Yossi and Yossi holding the boy. They swung him back and forth, threatening to send him flying into the sea of wild flowers. Zeke shrieked with delight.

It was past the regular season, but the unusually warm weather had kept crabs in the creek. At the dock, Zeke showed Yossi how to chicken-neck. He made him pull in the trot lines as he stood poised at the edge with a dip net. "No, Yossi, slower. Don't pull too fast. It's got to be like the crab feels the tide pulling on him, or he'll let go," he explained, Brian hearing the words he'd spoken last summer to him echoing now out of his mouth, his son's mind like the claws of that crab holding stubbornly

43

onto the bait, not letting any tidbit go, ever, not the word suck nor the name of every character in *The Chronicles of Narnia*, nor the nationality the word torturer had become tied to on news segments only heard peripherally, but leached into the air. His eye caught a flickering shadow just under the dazzle of light on the water and just then Zeke's net darted down and in and came up heavy and twitching with a crab. Zeke held it up in front of Yossi's face, then flipped it into the empty white paint can. The crab scuttled on the bottom, its claws raised at them.

"It's very ugly," Yossi said. "Like a, how do you say, *juke*, a cockroach."

"That's gross, Yoss," Zeke said.

Brian tapped the pole of the dip net in front of the crab; when it grabbed, Zeke reached quickly behind and pulled it up by a back fin. It was a large male, a jimmy, at least six inches between the horns of its shell, the lapis lazuli of its claws startling against the gleaming white underside. He twisted it in front of Yossi. "See, it's a male, Yossi," Zeke said. "See the belly—that's the Washington Monument. The girls have the Capitol dome on their bellies."

"Go ahead and pull up the pot," Brian said. "Yossi, you can set out a few more lines."

The crab pot dripped with jellyfish when Zeke hauled it out of the water, the shapes in it scuttling frantically as the wire cage came into the air, then settling down when it touched the dock, as if a curiosity about their fate had stilled the crabs. It was the same each time. Brian realized he was thinking of them as if they were like the personified creatures from one of the books he read with Zeke at night. "Kill the crab, kill the crab," he heard his son chant. He agitated the cage. The crabs fell into a clicking, carapaced mass in one corner, their mouths bubbling and foaming, two with their claws gripping each other's shells and a cracking sound as the steady pressure broke through one, the two crabs staying motionless, locked together and killing each other with the pressure of fear as they waited to be killed. "Kill the crab, kill the crab," Zeke sang, and Brian saw, his heart sinking, a shell that wasn't crab, its top faceted and symmetrical. He took the pot from Zeke, released the stretched rubber tie holding the top edges together and shook the crabs out into the bucket. The empty shell he'd spotted started to fall and he turned the edge away and let it fall onto the dock, along with one crab. The crab, a small one, scurried backwards towards the water, its claws raised at them. It fell in with a plop. "Look at this, Zeke," he said.

It was the nearly emptied, beautifully patterned shell of a diamond back terrapin. The turtle must have crawled into, or been pulled into the pot. There were a few tendons of meat webbing the inside of the shell, but otherwise it had been picked clean by the crabs. In the summer, they'd see the turtles all over and sometimes in the car Zeke would yell, "Turtle patrol," and he would stop on the shoulder of the road and dash out into the highway to pick up one of the doofus, lumbering creatures, usually frozen in fear by the noise of the traffic, its head and legs pulled inside. What place did cars have in the turtles' mythology? What place did crabs have—some turtle horror movie he now saw playing in Zeke's glittering eyes as his son fingered the torn meat inside the shell, summarized it in a whispered *wow*: that fascination with gory forms of death that Zeke and all his friends had, this male thing Mary didn't understand of dying for, killing for, stamped now on his son's face, "Kill the crab, kill the crab," Zeke chanted, Yossi smiling and joining in with him. "Revenge for the turtle," Zeke shouted, and Brian thought how he'd taught him to painlessly dispatch crabs before steaming them; you flipped them over, pressed the point of a knife into the top of the tab, the Washington Monument or Capitol dome on their bellies, into their hearts. The restaurants did it sometimes to prevent the crabs from losing their claws during steaming; Brian did it because he couldn't stand their frantic clicking under the steamer lid, the thought of their pain. Zeke did it because he thought it was neat, asking eagerly to be allowed to stab the crabs, the death fascination, a curse of viciousness in his son that scared Brian into pomposity so that he'd delivered a stiff, off-putting lecture about killing only to eat. Yet sometimes Zeke was tender; turtle patroller, rescuer of a hurt cat from teasing boys, protector of Yossi.

"Kill the crab, kill the crab," Yossi and Zeke sang together, his son's face glowing with happiness and release.

Brian picked up the bucket and emptied the crabs into the holding cage floating next to the dock. He pulled in the trot lines, too hard, the tightness on one slackening as he jerked it.

"Come on," he said. "Let's get back."

"Aren't we going to take these?" Zeke said, disappointed.

"Yossi won't eat them anyway. Would you Yossi?"

"They're disgusting."

They walked back silently through the meadow. The meadow was anything but silent; it hummed and buzzed and whined in Brian's ears, shrill with the noise of insects, billions in one field, hunting, preying on each other, locked in combat; the meadow nested, waiting. Yossi stuck out his foot and tripped Zeke and Zeke fell, too heavily. He looked up, dazed, at Yossi, then laughed and jumped at him. Yossi caught him and flipped him upside down. "You rat," Zeke yelled. He got up. As he ran towards Yossi, Brian stuck out his foot and Zeke fell again. "Yossi and Yossi—two jerks," he said, his voice going a little shrill. Brian pulled him up, then turned his hip into Zeke's chest and yanked down on one arm, grabbed him under the armpit and flipped him, a movement still automatic in his muscles after all these years, executed easily on the light body of a child. "Kill the kid, kill the kid," he sang. "You rat, Dad," Zeke yelled and Brian flipped him again, Zeke falling heavily and up and charging, not laughing now, and Brian put him down again, watching his son's body fall hard into the bushes and he picked him up and slammed him again. Now when Zeke's face came up, scratched from the brush, Brian saw there were tears streaked on his cheeks and he understood, his heart falling with a sick weight, he understood from where the danger he feared, dug himself in against, uncovered over and over in the earth, came. He caught Yossi's eye and saw his own panic understood and reflected, Yossi

46

and Yossi, both of them named for a man whose right hand had withered, whose arm had frozen in response to its capacity for violence.

"You hurt me," Zeke yelled.

Brian picked him up and tried to hold his squirming body, patted his legs and back. "It was an accident. Where's it hurt?"

Zeke jerked away. He was still crying.

"Get away. Soft nuts. Daddy dumb." He kicked at Brian. Brian held him tighter.

"It was an accident, buddy."

"No it wasn't. Let me go, you dork, you abuser. You don't treat me right."

Yossi was staring, his face blank and passive, his mouth slightly agape. Brian stroked Zeke's hair. "I wouldn't hurt you, buddy, not for the world; you know that. I wouldn't let anything hurt you."

"You hurt me." Brian looked at Yossi. His Israeli cousin was staring at him silently and then Zeke, sobbing, came into his arms. They rocked together, holding onto each other in helpless alliance against the buzzing insistence of the field.

BACK IN THE WORLD

I KNOCK. THE DOOR opens. Minh stares at me like he doesn't believe it. *Trick or treat.* This girl dust drifting onto his backsteps. He's wearing only a pair of striped pajama pants, big belly hanging over the waistband. The woman next to him is in a bathrobe. She tightens the belt. Minh says something to me.

"No speakee," I say.

"What are you doing here, Kiet?" he says in English.

The woman steps back and lets me inside. I never been in a real Vietnam home, people who still have the real in their minds instead of movie flickers. I look around for something that will pin my heart. Ancestors in square hats and high collar silk pajama clothes, women dressed like Whoopee Goldberg on *Star Trek* look through me from framed photos on a little table in the corner, the same way the woman stared at me. She lights an incense stick in front of them. From somewhere, another room, I hear something cry, a part of me trapped somewhere in here. Down a hall, in a locked room.

"What happened to that place where you were staying?" Minh asks me. "The home for girls?"

"Nothing."

He walks over to me, the friendly fat man I met before gone, tilts my head up: I'm the magic eight-ball and the answers to all his questions are going to swim into view in my eyes. Yes. No. Absolutely not. "The police will be after you," he says.

I shrug. "So what, man. I'm the last VC."

"Fuck the VC," Minh says. Then softens. "Listen, I'd like to help you. But there's nothing I can do."

"Nothing for dust."

"We're all dust in this country, little sister. But I can't afford the trouble. And you may be better off to stay in that place—it's a roof over your head."

Minh calling me little sister makes something turn over in me, something to do with this room and its smells.

The woman leaves and comes back with a plate heaped with rice and spicy beef. She smiles and gestures at me to sit and eat. Her smile or my hunger makes me a little dizzy and weird. I sit on the sofa and scoff the food down.

"I can't stay there."

The woman says something sharply.

"She wants to know," Minh says, "you remember your mama, where you come from?"

I turn and look at her.

"You don't remember nothing?" Minh says.

"When I see a movie, a Vietnam movie, sometime I remember. I think I remember."

"Bullshit," he snaps, his anger surprising and then delighting me. There's a shivery interest in the woman's eyes too, like she's looking at me more closely now.

So I tell them how sometimes a picture will blow into my head as a memory off the glowing screen. This scene, the GI's go into the village and there's a scar-faced sergeant picks out a woman, with her little girl watching all this, and he puts his gun to her head and screams at her, like where's the VC, bitch? and she screams back until he just blows her away. Just to stop all her annoying noise. And I can feel that barrel pressed against my mind. And I know that was how my real Ma died and I was the little girl watching.

And I know it's all true. The truth in direct opposite to all bullshit what they told me in all my foster homes and group homes about me leaving there when I was just a little baby with some family used my skin and hair as a ticket. That nobody knew who my real mother was. Watching the movie I knew it was true that I was the little girl who screamed and cried and watched her mama shot and laying dead among the pigs. The same skin covers us both. I know beyond doubt. I know even I don't remember a color of that place except colors the movies put in my head. And I think, looking at Minh, if I can't tell you who can I tell and don't you tell me no weak American shit, like it's only a movie, or I born too late and come out too dark, shit the counselors said.

Minh looks back at me a long time.

What I want to tell him with every part of my soul is: Let me stay here. Be a part of this Vietnam home, the faces on the wall slowly softening as they get to recognize me.

The woman sits down next to me and takes one of my hands. I thought she might have been Minh's wife or girlfriend, but closer I see she's a lot older than him. She looks into my eyes, but speaks in Vietnamese to Minh.

"What'd she say?"

"She doesn't speak English, but she understands it. She understands you, Kiet. You listen to her. She says you're looking for your Vietnam soul. And it's looking for you. But she says the scar-faced Sergeant is a *tinh*. Trying to deceive you."

A chill runs through me. The woman squeezes my hand.

"Do you know about Vietnam ghosts?" Minh asks.

I eat more, trying not to look at him or her. "I know their name. *Ma*."

"There are many kinds of ghosts, Kiet. *Ma, quy, tinh, tien, con hoa, yeu*. Some are good. The ghosts of ancestors who have been honored. Lucky spirits like *tien*. But some talk people into killing themselves by whispering *co, co*, neck, neck, into their ear until they get the idea, hang themselves. Some are the ghosts of the drowned that can't rest until they drown another to take their place. So they wait near the water and say: so cold here. But what she's talking about, *Tinh*, they try to make you open your mouth so they can suck out your soul and leave you fucking mad. The scar-faced Sergeant, he's just a picture, girl, you understand, a picture of a *tinh* come into your mind. She says you must keep looking for your soul, little sister, and for your mother's soul, and for your father's too. But you must stay away from the wrong ghosts."

*　　*　　*

I watch the line of Americans break up into fat green drops that ooze through the bamboo stalks. The drops move through the tall grass that borders the village. Elephant grass. I hear curses as the sharp blades whip back into their faces. Waste the place. Waste it and go back to the World. They come into the red mud clearing in front of my hootch, scrunching up their faces like each step hurts them. Maybe their boots are new. But they're old. Hair scraggly under their helmets. Skins yellowy-white and sweaty. Panting. Tongues hanging out. One comes and stands in front of me, his shadow falling on me and my baby. I shiver. My baby shivers against my skin. He takes off his helmet and wipes his scarred face. Sweat and blood flowing and pulsing in the map of scars. He sneers at my straw hootch, then what he does, he leans over and licks the side of it with a red pointy tongue. He looks down at me. I hold my baby tight to my breasts. You VC, girl? he asks. What about the brat? What's the kid, dink or splib? I throw my baby at him. It explodes with a flash and a loud bang. Bangs and flashes jump from the GI's rifles. They burn into my breasts and thighs.

Something is biting me.

I open my eyes and I'm back in the World.

I think: Minh's house. But Minh had sent me on my way. Chao ong, *Kiet. Drop us a line. Remember our kindness, you win the revolution. Otherwise don't come back.*

Tall pine trees above me. Bugs crawling over me.

I get up, pull down my pants, squat and pee. A cold breeze

whistling up my bottom. My horse stream spattering the leaves. I let out a nice rich happy morning fart, and sigh. Only I don't know if it is morning, how long I slept. No sun. The sky is gray through the bare branches. I can hear the river flowing nearby. Build me a raft, find Jim, do some shit with him never crossed Hucky Fuck's crimped redneck brain. Or maybe it did. Reading that book, sixth, no seventh grade: Huck and Jim lying naked on that raft, floating down the river like they were cut loose of everything. Then I see them coming through the trees. Not Huck and Jim. Like my dream. But no dream. Four of them. Only two of the four in uniform, one black guy one white guy. Only the uniforms just regular cop clothes. No helmets, no M-16s, just the heat in their holsters. But like the dream anyway 'cause for sure they must be after me. Out on a Kiet hunt. Find the last VC. I cut off my stream, freeze.

They're walking along the skinny beach. Cold wind whistling off the water. Their pants flapping against their legs. Walking with the exact same space between them, like so one grenade couldn't get them all. I look at their faces. They're old enough to have been there, slid right out of my dream. Except one guy walking kind of behind them, who looks foreign, like he's not easy here in his body, his clothes, this place. He's younger, but that's not it. Like he's with them but not of them. Short black hair and black eyes that rake the woods where I'm standing. I pull up my pants and start moving with them, a little behind, screened by the trees, by the wind noise. The VC tactics my Ma would have used. Be their own shadow. Hug the belt buckle of the enemy. Right. Done *that* before, Ma. How bout you? Of course another movie comes into my head now. Real movie (they're all real), real village they wiped out. No lie. That the name of the place. No Lie. Put the people in a ditch, blew them away, though what I remember, one GI wouldn't shoot the people in the ditch but he go find some young girl, put a pistol to her head, make her give him a blow job. In the middle of it all. His pants around his knees. Maybe his scuz filtering down into her stomach, through the thin womb wall. Making mutant me.

Tonetta told me that could happen. She'd know. Maybe he was one of these four, that guy in the movie. He wasn't a black dude though, so he couldn't be my real dad. Sure as shit could be one of my foster perverts though. Not a doubt. No lie.

The black cop stops, looks back and up towards me. I become one with the fucking trees. Their black shadow. He frowns. Goes on. I breathe again. One of those black guys was at the village said he shot one woman running, shot her and the baby in her arms. Went nuts, shot everybody after that, cut off body parts, all that. Like after the baby there couldn't be nothing worse so he could do anything. Or like he was trying to find if there was something worse. See how far he would go. Now there he was in this little room, sitting and shaking, showing the reporter or whoever this scar-book, pictures of what they done to that place. I know the name isn't scar-book. Like it was his family pictures. Never went out of the room. He'd put himself in prison. Sat and looked at the pictures and popped pills from all these bottles lined in front of him like lines of soldiers moving through a village. His hands shaking like that old boxer, Muhammed Ali. He looked like Muhammed Ali. He said he'd had a kid but the kid was shot in a drive-by, like it was payback. But it must not have been, cause he didn't look like he thought anything was even. This is my life, he said.

Absolutely. Life in the box. Know what you mean, bro.

"Right ahead," the older non-cop white guy yells.

He stops next to a little red flag. I get down, crawl close enough to see, hear. There's a line of the little flags, around a roped-off area in front of a little cliff. Only its part of the same bank I'm on, only folded around from where I lay so I can see it from the side. The earth in the cliff is red and wet and looks like skin. Roots coming out of it like fat slimy veins. The part of the beach they're standing around is covered with a blue kind of shiny plastic cover.

Standing in front of it without talking, staring. Maybe they're not looking for me.

56

"You got it marked off like a murder scene," the black cop says.

"SOP," the other guy says. "Our jobs are pretty much the same in that sense. Time of death, cause of death. I look into the crime. Only I don't need to worry about punishment."

He squats down and takes the rocks off the corners of the covers and pulls it away. The other two squat down next to him. On their heels. Like the pictures in the scar-books. I'm sure they've been there. I look, then look again to be sure of what I'm seeing. It's true. Scattered everywhere, pushing out of the ground like they've tunneled here from the other side of the earth, just like me.

"Or justice," the black cop says. He nods at the bones. "The only good rebel."

The white cop grins at him in a way that makes me shiver. There was a skull went with those heaped bones, it would have that grin. "Is that what these are?"

The foreign guy says nothing. He's staring right where I'm at. He closes his eyes like he's afraid he saw something he shouldn't, past the veil of air.

"I'm fairly sure these are remains from the prison camp period, just from a superficial look at them," the other man says. He sounds like a teacher. "But there could be more than one man, a few mixed up. I found some Union army uniform buttons nearby."

"How do you know they're his," the white cop says.

"I can't be a hundred percent sure—there's often a mixture of artifacts in this area. And remains: these might be a mixture of more than one set of remains—prisoner, guard, more, who knows. I'm not basing my opinion solely on the juxtaposition of the button to the disinterred," Teacher says.

"Only on the angle of the dangle," White Cop says.

"Disinterred," Black Cop says. He says the word like it hurts his mouth. "Mixed. Desegregated. Disinterred and desecrated. Disturbed."

Teacher doesn't like it, turns and looks at him in a kind of hurt but sarcastic, Teacher way.

"A disturbance," White Cop says.

Teacher looks at him next. Disturbed. "Anything on the runaway girl?" Teacher asks. Like that. Like somehow White Cop's word had brought me up. Like I'm the secret in the woods they whisper about.

"We've had reports that she's been seen right around here, at Point Lookout," Black Cop says. He squats and touches one of the bones, runs his finger along it in a way that runs a shiver across my skin, under my skin; it's my bones he's caressing. "Brief, cryptic messages from Listening Posts past the perimeter. Sightings. Vague green forms flitting here and there in the night scopes. Glimpses. Rumors and reports. She may be watching us even as we speak." His eyes sweep up and down the woods, brush over me like a cold hand.

"Like I told you," he says, "She owns the night."

He's wrong. Night owns me. Listen. This is why I'm telling you all this. You blind. So I know you can see what I saw that night, after they left. The darkness swelling inside my head. Nibbling on my cheeks like the place was charged with something. The darkness pressing against my eyes like fingers. Flutterings. Whisperings. Lappings. Noise drawing shapes on my skin. Shapes peeling and sliding off my skin and forming out in the darkness. Thickenings. Listen. Look. As if I'm giving you sight. But I'm taking your dark too. So that what we both have now is twilight. So that the light will never be more or less than this. So that the shapes will never be clear. So I can never see the twisted faces. Moon scraps broken on the water like something breaking up inside me. The ground under my patting fingers feels hollow. Tunnels underneath. The moonlight blurring a piece of the darkness like an eraser smear which turns into a boat moving silent along the shore. Shouts and murmurs coming from it. Whispered secrets. Glimpses. Rumors and reports. The bone

WAYNE KARLIN

white beach sucks the water to it. A splash that echoes in my
head, the cold water sloshing around heavy inside my skull,
pushing against my eyes. I touch the bones. *This is my flesh,*
someone says. *You must keep looking for your soul, little sister,
and your mother's soul, and your father's too,* someone says. In
my head but outside my head. I'm a mixture of artifacts. My
hands touching the mixed disinterred disturbed dink and splib
bones. *Eat me.* I lick one, taste mud and salt. A cold dirty cell
moving into me. Garble, garble, garble, the voices say. Only I
have the words for them now, words put into my head by Minh's
woman. *Co, co,* the voice says. Neck, neck. Chu-chu-cha-choo.
My fingers touching the bones. *Ma, quy, tinh, tien, con hua, yeu.*
Which said one way means love. Ee-oh. Which said another way
means ghost. *Yeu.*

Me—oh.

PRISONERS

THE WEEK HAD KEPT turning corners that left Russell facing the past. Yesterday, interrogating a twenty year old white male named Jason Waxman who was suspected of dealing crack cocaine at the high school, he had inadvertently joked in Vietnamese with Trung, a California-born deputy. Trung had looked at him blankly: he affected not to speak a word. But the suspect had gone pale at the sound of the language. "You're a vet," he had said.

Russell found himself offended at the boy's fear.

"What are you, a cocker spaniel? You need to be altered?"

"You know what I mean."

He had put Waxman's thumb between his own thumb and forefinger, the boy's flesh white as bone against his skin. At the gentle squeeze he gave, Waxman began to talk. He was scared to death. Russell had learned long before that being offended by a stereotype didn't mean you shouldn't use it.

Now he was driving to Point Lookout to help in the search for a sixteen year old half-black, half-Vietnamese girl named Kiet who had run away from a residential program for troubled adolescent girls.

He was taking his time. He doubted that Kiet would come in this direction; usually when girls went AWOL from the counselling center they headed north, to DC or Baltimore. But a figure, female, had been spotted wading out at the Point, and the cold water was being dragged and searched by divers.

The girls, often inner-city kids, hated being sent to the boonies, and where he was now was the least populated area of

63

the county: a crust of houses, white clapboard churches and country stores along the highway, beyond them fields and forest and marsh. The further south you went, the narrower the peninsula became until finally the Potomac and the Bay pinched out the land between them; that tip of the county was Point Lookout. The state had started from here, back in 1634, and so, in a sense, had he: the progenitor of his own family—a slave named Lucius from Dahomey via Barbados, had come with the British ship Ark to this place, bought by a carpenter named Hallam: a fact Russell's boss Alex Hallam, white, that man's descendent, regarded with an amusement that Russell didn't know how to take.

Alex believed, Russell knew, that he was spiked and fastened by his obsession with family history. But he didn't believe he had the choice Alex implied. He had been born, like many in his family, with twelve fingers; the extra two had been amputated when he was a baby. But he still felt the invisible ache of them on his hands, organs of an extra sense that dipped and stirred into time. Time touched him back. It wasn't a matter of searching it out. It was simply there, the weight of an internal presence. It was something the Vietnamese would probably understand: their ancestry and history were felt as points of reference, of lookout, in a person's soul. Though Kiet, the child he was looking for, black GI father she never knew, Vietnamese mother, only had a history of running away.

He was nearly at the beginning of the state park now. On impulse, he stopped at the memorial to the Confederate dead, an obelisk with the names of the dead inscribed on copper plates fastened around its base. Over thirty-five thousand prisoners had been kept at the Point Lookout camp, some of them rebel sympathizers from the county. Thousands of men had died here, of disease, exposure, maltreatment. The prisoners had been packed into flimsy tents and slept on the ground: the country was marshy and unhealthy and exposed to ill winds off the Chesapeake Bay and the river. Many must have died, he supposed, of broken hearts: to the west, on the Potomac side, they would have stood and stared at the shoreline of Virginia, as distant and as tantalizing as the shores of heaven. He imagined it added to their sense of hell that often their guards were ex-slaves who had joined the Union army: the prisoners' and in fact the Union officers' diaries that he had read expressed horror that black troops had been set over Confederate prisoners. His family had a story about an ancestor who had been a guard and who had either abused or murdered a white Hallam, his former master. He had never been able to confirm the story in any of the histories. Perhaps it was only wishful thinking.

In Vietnam, when he had briefly been a guard at a POW compound himself, he had tried to relate the experience to Point Lookout. But the Vietnamese prisoners, mostly starved amputees, were poor substitutes for white Southerners, and the job had only caused him to lose the romantic image he had of the VC as supermen. Their filth, lethargy and indifference had infuriated him. When he knew he'd murder someone if he had to keep looking at their faces, he'd gotten a transfer back to a line unit.

The mist draped around the monument and paled the bright green of the pines behind the iron-picket fence that enclosed the area. A moldy smell clogged his nostrils and the cone of air around him turned suddenly icy, a spot he could move out of, he found, by taking a step to the right or left. He wondered if it were a trick of air currents or if his presence had stirred something.

He walked to the needle, put his hand down flat, over some names. The coldness of the metal moved into his palm. He had been once, only once, to the Wall in Washington. Standing at its apex, he had felt he was winging out from his own center, the names carved inside him. He couldn't stay. But the names on this monument, even the familiar county names his fingers traced now, meant nothing to him. More than nothing: he was glad they were dead.

He looked for Hallam, as he had before, but again he couldn't find his own name on the monument.

He left the memorial and drove south, passing the signs for the camping ground and Civil War museum, set back in the tall loblolly pines to the right of the narrow road. On the other side were several weather-beaten frame houses, their yards weedy, the knobbed silver globe of a sea-mine on a pedestal in one front yard. Then the country opened suddenly, and it was as if he were driving into water, passing from one element to the other, the road on top of a narrow stone berm, the Bay vast and gray and seething with white caps on his left, Lake Conoy, a large pond that flowed into the Potomac on his right. He could see the river glinting through a thin tall picket of loblollies on the eastern edge of the pond. At the end of the causeway, on the Bay side, was a brief wedge of grass between the road and the water. A spoked iron wheel stood half-buried near a picnic table. He stopped the car again, stalling, not sure why.

He got out. A boy was standing on the edge of the rocks near the grass, throwing a baited line out into the water. It was the wrong time of year for crabs, but the boy's concentrated stillness tugged a memory out of Russell; when he was a kid, crabbing, he would stand like that, a dip net in one hand, the other delicately holding the end of a trot line, pulling his thoughts from the gray flowing of the water. He touched the iron of the wheel, wondering if it were an object from the camp. It held a different coldness than the monument's: the coldness of the water in which it had lain. The land had steadily eroded since the prison had been here; during the war the shoreline here extended out perhaps half a mile into the Bay. On the horizon, he saw a ship, a freighter headed towards Baltimore, drawing a line between sky and sea. He looked at the near water. It was cold and dark and smoothly heavy, heaving itself up, pushing against the shore.

Under the surface here would be more ruins, broken plates, chains, mini-balls, the barnacle-encrusted bones of unburied white prisoners clicking against the bones of the Middle Passage that had marched here along the ocean's bottom compelled to complete their journey, to push blindly against the mass of the continent. He tried to imagine the girl, Kiet's face, emerging suddenly, half-black, half- Vietnamese, his own past made into a construct, rising, water streaming from eye sockets and astonished mouth. A shadow passed under his gaze; he started, then grinned at himself as he recognized the surprisingly graceful flap and glide, a glimpsed motion that gave his imagination just enough to fill in the form of the ray. He let himself glide under the surface with it, the cold water smooth over him, his bottom eyes probing the dark rocks and silt, a sediment thick with secrets and crimes, his slit ears straining to hear voices, the stories, the one unknown story still held locked like another bone in the bottom mud. A distinct word, rose and opened in his mind, as perfectly as a bubble.

Hallam.

* * *

I AM CONSIDERED an educated man for one of my race, although Dr. Miles Oberle, my former mentor at the New England Conservatory for Freed Africans would undoubtedly chide me for the above phrase. You are simply an educated man, he would say. I have found, however, that while simplicity is much to be desired, it is rarely achieved and the qualification I make perhaps stems from the way I have come to regard myself. For if one thinks of education as enlightenment, of light, the pure *lux* (from the Greek *leukos*, white) which overcomes darkness then I cannot help but think of myself as that which must be overcome.

Lux et logos. Those gilted words, engraved above the door of Dr. Oberle's study, his sanctum sanctorum, will always conjure the Conservatory to me. *Lux* illuminated *logos. Lux* was the cool New England light that flowed like a blessing through the bay windows and touched a muted gleam from the polished oak furniture and floors, that awakened a warm smell, like that emanating from milk-fed, content animals nuzzling in a clean barn, from the leather-bound books lining the shelves. *Lux* glittered from the golden titles branded onto their spines. At certain times of the day, rainbow prisms of light would sparkle from the fine crystal in the red China closet, while at others, globules of lemony light would move like luminous spirits over the portraits of the Fathers, Washington and Jefferson, framed on the walls, decoalesce and drip onto the blindly staring marble busts of the great thinkers: Socrates, Plato, Aristotle, Descartes. That room was to me the physical formulation of logos itself. Even the mahogany fireplace mantelpiece, which was decorated with a bas relief of elephants and gilded Negro heads, their widened eyes gleeful with stupidity, their thick-lipped mouths, drooped open like idiot children's, seemed contained, made ridiculous and safe by the room, which of course was Dr. Oberle's intent in having it there. The design, he told me, was copied from the decoration over the door of the Liverpool Customs House and was emblematic of the slave trade: it was commonly said by the English themselves in those days that Liverpool's streets were marked out by chains, the bricks of its houses cemented with African blood. This too is conquered, Oberle wanted the decoration to say, conquered by the fact he dared put it there, conquered by what surrounded it: those paintings, those sculpted heads, the reasoned words standing in tight-shouldered solidarity on the book shelves. I found it impolitic to mention the obvious paradox that the right hand, so to speak, could sculpt one set of heads while the left carved those repulsive visages.

He was after all, my mentor. I had come to the Conservatory soon after I ran away from south Maryland in March of 1858, in my seventeenth year. In May of that same year, I had been asked to address an Abolitionist meeting on Boston Common, a gathering attended by Dr. Oberle. My quick tongue was married to my thick ignorance, a combination which drew him to me; I suppose I seemed backwards enough to benefit from his aid, yet gifted with enough natural eloquence to promise his success. At his request, we were introduced after the rally; he asked me if I could read and write (I could. Even though it was illegal, I had been taught the art at my old master's bidding, for he liked to have me read to him in the evenings). Soon after that interview, Oberle invited me to join the dozen or so other students, all runaway slaves, he had chosen to bring to the light.

For the most part, I remember my time at the Conservatory with fondness; it was a flowing and tranquil passage. There are only two incidents that jar my memory. The first occurred, of all places, in Bible class. I cannot be certain why that occasion has stayed in my mind except that it marked an unusual agitation in me about a subject which had never been one I had taken with any seriousness before, my mind tending towards the rational and scientific. That day Dr. Oberle was visiting the class, which was taught by the Reverend Silas Gough; the subject was Abraham begetting a child in his old age. According to Dr. Gough, faith in the possibility of the miraculous was one message we could extract from this incident.

But what of Ishmael, I found myself asking, my voice to my surprise, to the astonishment of the others in the room (Dr. Gough stroking his beard, looking at Dr. Oberle, who stroked his own in a mirroring response), suddenly cracking with emotion. I had learned by then—I was near graduation—to affect a dispassionate coolness sharpened with just an edge of sarcasm as my persona, and the rage that seized me was, to say the least, unexpected. How could a father abandon his own child, and that child's mother, to what he surely must have thought would have been certain death in the desert, simply because Ishmael was the child of a slave? I demanded. Was he not still Abraham's son. Only, to my further consternation, I realized I had not phrased my question in these words; in my agitation I slipped back into myself. "He not be Abraham chile?" I asked. Stopping myself, looking at the startled faces around me, looking startled myself at the words that had slipped past my lips like traitors, I suddenly realized that I had risen to my feet and was shouting.

I sat down, shamefaced, my hands trembling. The extended point of the passage, Mr. Hallam, Dr. Gough said quietly, is that this miracle made Abraham the progenitor of the Hebrews, who thus could fulfill their mission of becoming the human progenitors of the Christ, the light of the world. If Abraham's blessing had gone to Ishmael, this symbolically would signify the victory of the baser forces of his nature that had resulted in the child of the lower state. Yet to leave a child in the desert, I began, but stopped when I saw the impatience clouding his face, the disappointment in the eyes of Dr. Oberle. There is always the danger, Mr. Hallam, he said, of losing one's objectivity.

That Bible class had been my last before graduation and for a time I worried that my indiscretion might threaten my being chosen as valedictorian. But it did not.

Commencement took place in Dr. Oberle's study. There were but twelve of us in Dr. Oberle's graduating class that year, and to a man we enlisted in the 36th United States Colored Infantry, under Colonel A.G. Draper. I began my speech by announcing that enlistment with a beaming pride that produced a ripple of emotion from my audience. We needed, I said, as we went forth to battle, to recall that we were going to be engaged in a conflict unlike any other fought in the history of mankind, a struggle engendered not from greed, not from the coveting of a neighbor's goods and chattels, nor even from a desire to break the chains of tyranny from oneself, like the struggles of the slave Spartacus or the valiant Hasmoneans. No, I maintained, here, for the first time in human history, was a battle motivated by the purest altruism, for what else could we name it when the men of one race were willing to give their lives, to fight their own brothers, in order to liberate those of another race?

As we took our position in the ranks, I admonished, when the applause had ceased, we needed to nourish our astonishment at this sacrifice in order to save ourselves from the monster of vindictive hatred that could destroy us, even in our moment of victory. We, the sons of Ham, had eaten the bitter herbs of slavery, yet—we needed to remember—without that original taste, we would not be here either: the light of *logos* would have been denied us if we'd remained in our baser, native state, exiled in the desert. White hands had rudely plucked us from that state,

I said, my metaphors becoming somewhat confused in my excitement at the approval my speech was gaining; white hands had placed us in harsh servitude, yet white hands also—I nodded to the audience—had reached down and picked us up to the sun of truth and civilization. Thus, even as we fought our oppressors, we must never forget to guard against becoming like them through blind hatred and the facile satisfaction offered by retribution. In the words of Thomas Paine, I concluded, (I knew my audience) tyranny, like hell, is not easily conquered.

As I spoke, I kept my eye on Dr. Oberle, the faculty, the trustees of the institute. Their murmurs of approval, their pale hands stroking their beards with increasing speed, as if to gauge an inner pleasure, warmed me. In a theatrical manner even the day itself joined the ceremony: a beam of light flowed through the windows, illuminating, as if to paint into my memory, the details of that room. It fell on the shelves of books, it fell on the Persian carpet, on the richly gleaming oak furniture and then, inevitably, it fell on that accursed mantelpiece.

As the row of wooly headed, mocking faces suddenly blazed before my eyes, each became a black, metastasizing cell of doubt entering my body. These fathers nodding at me, these graybeards, had brought both of us to this room and I wondered suddenly at their intent in lining us before them, as into crooked mirrors. They had brought us into their light, these white men, but they had also fashioned these heads, we were both their children and neither of us their inheritors. Was this truly such a mystery to me, who knew it in my flesh that a hand that could caress and stroke could also rend and tear? Those gaped mouths called to me: who do you think you are, pickaninny, parrot, gibbering ape, what do you think you are doing here? I tried to force my gaze from them, but I turned my head and they melted into the faces of the faculty and trustees, faces suddenly anxious at my silence, mouths suddenly murmuring with concern instead of approval, and the metamorphosis continued so that I saw black flesh fall away and their whiteness became a row of grinning skulls that parodied the mocking African faces.

Finally, the growing mutter caused me to shake my head, shake off the vision, and I continued. But the applause when I finished my speech was more an outburst of relief than of admiration.

My graduation from the conservatory merged into a different form of education, that of the training camp, but I cheerfully endured its mindless brutality for I felt it was suffered to hone me for a nobler purpose. The earlier lessons of my slavery, which for the main part consisted of a protective retreat into expected mannerisms, came back to me at this time; they were of great value in my intercourse with my drill sergeant and white officers. At the end of our training period, we were read the news of the great scrap at Gettysburg and we became fearful the war would be over soon. I was wild with impatience, eager not to miss the tide of history.

To my disappointment, though, the 36th did not march to be tested in the crucible of battle. Instead, we were to be sent to Southern Maryland, the very place where I had endured my slavery, the cursed ground where I had buried my mother and promised myself not to return. But I was a soldier now; I had willingly sacrificed the freedom I'd taken to myself in order to extend and ennoble it. I had to, to put it simply, follow orders. The whites of the region, certainly not to my surprise, were sympathetic to the Secesh, and Federal troops that had to be sent to occupy the area both in order to catch blockade runners and also to control the spies and saboteurs this poisonous pocket of rebellion spewed northwards. In addition, a large prison depot had been built at Point Lookout just miles south of Scotland, where I had spent my years of servitude and we were to help garrison it. Although the Second regiment of New Hampshire Volunteers was already deployed at the depot, its population was growing due to the Confederacy's defeat at Gettysburg. And perhaps it was felt (although perhaps it could be the War Department was reluctant to trust us in battle) that justice would be served by assigning a regiment of colored troops as guards of their former keepers.

And so, in the beginning of May in the year 1863, behind the flags of regiment and country, I marched as official and unrelenting as a debt back to the place where I was born. There was something of the dream about it: in my uniform, armed, I moved down into a land devastated as if by the fire of my hatred. Fields had gone to weed or were growing up in pine trees; dogs and cattle were running wild. When we came to Leonardtown, the county seat, the buildings were closed, their windows boarded, and bony pigs were rooting in the main street. There were very few people who came out to see us, though I looked into every white face as if peering into a mirror, searching for the one face I knew as I knew my own to form before my eyes. But we passed only old men and women who stared at our black faces as if we had marched out of their own uneasy dreams. Only old men and women: they kept the children and the young women hidden and their able menfolk had gone to Virginia to join the rebels.

We marched south, down through the St. Inigoes district, until we passed Scotland. It was a name that, before my eyes were opened to geography, had meant only this hot, lowland place to me.

The prison camp spread itself below Scotland and onto the Point, exposed to wind and water on that sandy spit. Before us were the neat dwellings of the guard regiments, the sturdily fashioned and well maintained administrative and supply buildings and then, beyond them, a deadline ditch, a rampart and a city of rotting white canvas tents, acres of tents so ragged in appearance that they had the aspect of patches of diseased skin, scaling off the land. They covered the country of my childhood.

What I have kept all these years since is a stink in my nostrils and pictures, daguerreotypes fastened behind my mind's eye, flash burned into my brain. Pictures. A group of emaciated prisoners arriving at the wharf, my fellow guards, ex-slaves ennobled by their suffering, tearing the rags from the backs of these wretches and throwing that clothing into the Bay, so these white men stood naked in the wind, as on an auction block or an African beach. The malodorous mud alleys between the tents, puddled with urine and piled with lumps of excrement. A Negro guard shooting a squatting, bare-bottomed prisoner driven into the night by the diarrhea all of them had. A stocky, sturdy New Hampshire man shooting down with cold rage a Confederate officer who taunted him that Yankees and niggers, all guards, all in the same uniform, must be equal. Shooting him for the utterly offensive insult of that remark, this New England soldier on my side of the war. Another prisoner, a gaunt, bearded man with fiery eyes, a patriarchal figure who reminded me of lithographs I had seen of John Brown, stepping deliberately into the deadline ditch and Jim Tanner, the ex-field slave from Mississippi who had dared him to do it, just as deliberately shooting him in the head. Tanner. Tanner making prisoners driven from their tents by dysentery get on their knees and pray "fo President Lincoln and the colored folks," making them carry him on their backs as he whooped, his mud-stained, red-rimmed eyes rolling at me, fixed to mine, smiling his mockery at my look of disgust, his face one of the faces I had seen on the mantelpiece. Tanner.

He was my guide into this new country that my old country had rolled over into as if in some inexorable balancing of nature's justice. On my first day, he brought me with him into the prisoners' area. The prisoners scurried out of his way, disappearing into their tents as he walked the mud streets. Tanner was Provost Marshal Brady's favorite; he had gotten away with murder more than once, and they knew it. As we walked, he recited information about the layout of the camp, the rules involving relief of guard, the deadline, the contraband market (yes there was commerce in hell, surely no surprise to a former slave. I have heard that Major Brady, called Beast, left the Point with over a million dollars in his retirement fund). The prisoners, Tanner told me, were permitted twelve ounces of hard bread a day; if they had greenbacks they could always buy more. Or they could scavenge.

"It seems hardly enough for a man to live on, sergeant," I said.

Tanner turned to me. The weave of tiny veins that formed a scraggly red border around his eyes seemed to glow (old blood-eye the prisoners, and many guards for that matter, called him, when he was not within hearing). A slow smile spread on his face. "Why you talk so white, nigger?" he asked.

"I have had schooling," I said stiffly.

He laughed. When he spoke, he seemed to exaggerate the discrepancies of his language. "Well, le'me tell you somephin, School. Lose some sixty a day, fum de scurvy. We got bowt twenty-thousand take care ob. Scurvy too damn slow." He peered at me curiously. "I just gib dem dey amount. Set dey amount. You know about de amount, boy? Where you slave?"

"Here."

He laughed even louder. But the red glow stayed in his eye, smoldering like a choice he kept at hand under the choice he seemed to have made of being amused at me.

"Firs' day, field handin, I mus be six, seben year ol', dey gib me a sack," Tanner said. "Got a strap roun my neck, my mowth open, mowth a de sack open at my heart, bottom a de sack drag de ground. Also got dis basket, for when de sack full. Dey say pick, I pick. I pick, dey whip all de time fus day, cause what I doing, I settin my amount. Dat day my amount one hunnert pound. Dey nevah see no six, seben year old do one hunnert pound. Dat day on, at end a picking ebery day, you go down the Gin House, weigh up. Undah you amount, dey whip you up. Obah you amount, dey figger you fake befo, whip you up too, next day you pick dat much. Understand, School? You wanna see mah back, times I ovah or undah mah amount?"

"I have an amount that I have carried also, sergeant," I said (what a pompous ass I was in those days). "But I believe we must be better than they are."

The red net glowed. "Bettah. You right dere, School."

He spun around. His quickness caught a man who had been standing in the shade of a tent, eavesdropping on our conversation. I had not thought that Tanner had seen him. The prisoner was still wearing the bedraggled uniform of a Confederate captain. He stared at us strangely. He had a long, thin face and his rotted teeth, elongated by the retraction of his gums, gave it a horse cast. He looked back and forth at our faces, then nodded and laughed to himself.

Tanner nodded also. "Come on ovah heah, Cap'n Norris," he said.

The man shrugged and pulled something from his pocket. He held it up in front of his face as he approached us, snapping it between his hands. A greenback. When his breath washed over me, I understood why he had not ducked back into his tent like the others.

"You look like a damned old whiskeyhead, sergeant," he said, swaying. "Why don't you take this, go buy me some whiskey. From your massa, the Beast. Go fetch me some beast whiskey. Some hairy beast brew."

When he was finished, he stood, a sneer forming on his lips, then disappearing, then forming, as if he were tugged between fear and insolence. As if a part of him were remembering to be afraid.

"Dis man talkin contraband, School," Tanner said. "You head him?"

"Sergeant, a little philanthropy is all I ask," Norris gave a mock bow. "Aren't you a philanthropist, sergeant? You look ripely philanthropic to me."

"You callin me what?" Tanner said, putting a hand behind his ear. A kind of calmness descended on his face.

"Captain Norris," I said, "why don't you take yourself out of here now."

Norris looked from Tanner to me, smiling and shaking his head as if he could not believe what was in front of his eyes.

Tanner drew his revolver from its case. I could feel that motion in my stomach also.

"Sergeant," I said quickly. "Philanthropist is not an insult."

He glanced at me, then back at Norris, and smiled. "Ain't no insult? You wrong, School. Philanthropist mean nigger, doan it, Cap'n?"

He pointed the revolver at Norris. Norris stiffened, then tore open his shirt. He rubbed his filthy chest, pointing to his heart, still swaying.

"Philanthropist," he said.

Tanner cocked the revolver and fired into Norris' chest. Norris flew backwards and fell into a tub that had been sunk into the mud as a latrine. I stood staring at the body, the greenback still clutched in one hand, waiting for him to get up, for the lesson to be over. The flies started gathering quickly; there were many already there. "That was cold murder," I said. But Tanner just smiled at me again, a conspiratorial smile, as if he had seen into my heart, sensed the surge of pure triumph and joy I had felt when he fired into that arrogant breast.

"Bettah," he said.

I open a tent flap, even now, in memory, in dreams, and the prisoners' faces turn to me slowly. A menagerie of the faces of my youth. Even now, in memory, in dreams, they must stay animalistic, for I can't bear think of them as men. Sly, fox-faces. Flat, snake-mean eyes that gleam with contempt, even as they opaque with fear. Bats in a cave, blinking awake. So many eyes. The tents are made to hold sixteen; we stuff in forty. Forty of them: high or low, thick or thin, though they all thinned and sharpened after a while, took on the smudged white and gray coloring of the tents as if they had become a new race. Not foxes nor snakes nor bats. Dogs. A doggish race that we kenneled, their wagging and hand-licking, their nipping at each other, their occasional snarls of defiance, their cur's stink. How they hated me. How I revelled in their hatred. How I hated them back. I raise my Sharps as Tanner had raised his revolver and I point it and I feel the freedom and the power that Tanner must have felt. If they had one head I would blow it off.

I spin around and leave that closed place, seeking air and light. I spin and spin.

Below the prison compound, surrounded by its deadline ditch and stockade, was the Hammond Hospital, a series of twenty buildings arranged like spokes in a circle. Twelve hundred patients could be held in its wards; there were over six thousand when I was at the Point. If the prisoners had become as dogs, then at Hammond the prison surgeons were another race also, a race with serrated, sharpened fingers, with strange hunger in its eyes. Among the Whydahs, I had read in a book I found once in Dr. Oberle's library, all sickness is thought to come from the curses of enemies: cure came from removing—removing first the curse and then the enemy. To those Whydah, the surgeons of Point Lookout, limbs were curses and their answer was removal also.

It was Tanner who brought me to Hammond, and Tanner of course who took me to the charnel tent, showing it to me like a choice he was putting into my mind, though I did not understand that until later. He pulled back the flap and grinned and stood to one side to let me look. The amputated legs and feet and arms were stacked neatly as cots or tent poles: legs on legs, feet fitted with feet, detached hands cupped, all their palms up. Flesh apple-fresh as stolen youth and flesh already rotted with death, moving with maggots, buzzed by obscenely fat bluebottle flies. Flesh that had blackened or browned, as if our color were contained within it. At the sight of that horrible uniformity my mind tilted and I thought: here they build us.

I fled both the sight and Tanner's laughter and rushed behind the tent. Doubling over, I released a stream of bile, then heaved and retched, my eyes fastened to the ground. Bent over in this posture, I saw the back edge of the tent rise slightly at its bottom, as if being nudged up, and then I screamed, for from that black gap came a scuttling line of detached hands, escaping, scurrying along the ground sideways, their fingers moving like legs. I reeled up and my eyes met Tanner's mocking, red-rimmed orbs. "What sicks you, boy?" he asked, and brought his heel down hard. I heard a terrible, crushing sound. We stood for a moment, our eyes locked, then I looked. Under Tanner's boot, its claws still clutching a trophy of torn flesh, was the good friend of my childhood, a Maryland blue crab, come up from the inlet that lapped near the tent to feast on the grabbers that for so long had pulled his friends and family from the water.

"Come on, School," Tanner said, "got somephin make you feel bettah."

Taking my arm, he led me away from the hospital to a section of the compound to which I had not yet been, to a tent that was identical to all the other tents. He smiled at me and opened the flap just as he had at the charnel tent.

I entered. The flap closing behind me closed me into a dream. A face I had sunken into the deepest depths of myself loosened from its weights and bobbed up, real and inescapable in front of my eyes.

"Private Hallam," Tanner said. "You find somephin you enjoy heah? Pass de time, say? Somephin bettah?"

I nodded, unable to speak.

"Yours," Tanner said simply.

There was no one else in the tent; the others must have been out on work parties. I walked towards the figure on the ground.

"Hallam," I said hoarsely, the sound of my own name in that rank, closed place startling to my ear.

"Hallam," I said again, as if to relieve myself of it, give it back to this skeleton who had given it to me.

He didn't move, only stared at me. If he recognized me, he refused to acknowledge it. As I looked at him, my eyes fastened like crab claws to his flesh, I remembered the day I had marched

79

back into the county and saw it scorched, as if from my wishes. His body was similarly devastated. The powerful form I remembered was wasted away. His hair was mostly gone, except for a few lank, filthy strands. His face was skullish, the skin yellowed and waxy. The padded, sloped strength of his shoulders, the muscles I had seen dancing under a gleam of sweat as he punished, as he hit or drove his need forward into my mother's body, had withered to wing bone. And his hands. These were not the calloused, vein-knotted pinchers I remembered: cunning fasteners and whittlers of wood, boat building hands, trot-lining hands, strokers, graspers, carvers, seizers, twisters, grippers of the handles of whips, of the heavy links of chains, carapaced scuttlers that moved like feeding creatures over the front of my mother's calico dress, patters of warm-waves of love into the top of my head that suddenly grabbed my face, pulled it close as if to a mirror and what he saw in that mirror blossoming on his face into disgust and self-loathing. Those hands.

They had been crushed as if under Sergeant Tanner's boot, the fingers skewed and splintered, black crescent moons where the nails were torn off, the skin as black as the flesh of the hands I had seen pleading at me in the charnel tent, black as if the name he had given me like a curse had come back to him from me. He raised those terrible claws to me. His cracked lips moved and he croaked, but the words were words I might have heard if I had just come into his bedroom of a Sunday morning to help him dress for church:

"Help me, boy."

Did he recognize me? I don't know. Even after I pressed my face to his, even after I called out my name and his crime, screamed it into his face, all he might have seen was another nigger guard calling him to his amount.

I pushed my rage back into my heart, a case that had hardened over the years to contain it.

"You need the hospital," I said.

At the word, a look of horror sprung onto his face. "No," he moaned. "Nooowhooo." It was the howl of a terrified dog.

"You'll die," I said.

"Help me," he whispered, looking into my eyes now as if he at last recognized me. "Feed me," he said.

The slaves in Southern Maryland prepare a ham in a way, my mother told me, that they brought from Africa: it was done both for the tastiness of it and to preserve the meat in hot weather. The negroes would take the pieces of butchered hog their owners would give them on holidays, groove the meat and then stuff the grooves with greens and peppers and mustard seeds. My mother had often prepared this dish for Hallam. It was our old master's favorite meal.

From the guards' garden then, and from some of the traitors that did business in the camp I gathered the ingredients: kale, cabbage, cress, turnip tops and wild onions. The ham I bought from an old negro man in Scotland, just north of the prison: he had lost his family when they were all hurriedly sold to Virginia before the Federal troops came into the area, and he was living with the pig in a little shack outside the abandoned quarters of his master. When I asked him why he didn't move into the main house, he looked at me as if I were a lunatic. He treated that pig with affection, as if it were a child, but he needed the greenbacks and I was willing to pay.

The other guards teased me as I began to prepare the dish, but when they saw my face they stopped and formed a silent circle around me. Silent at first, but after a time they began to mutter, a steady drone of voices that seemed to hum and vibrate in the bone of my skull. "...His mama...lak the ham...stuff hisself in, split fo sho...wah he do...see, see." I cut the greens and vegetables fine, and I chopped and I chopped, the salty drops of my sweat falling on them and then I put them into a tub, and I mixed in red pepper and salt and mustard seed while all around me and in me the voices droned. I took a clean cotton shirt and I cut it up the front, the guards moaning as the knife touched and split, see, see, and I lay it open on the table. Then I tenderly laid a bed of green on the cloth and turned to the ham. I took my bayonet and cut deep crescents into the pink, giving flesh, making a crisscross pattern, the point of the knife meeting the resistance of the flesh, then my thrust breaking through, the moan around and from me increasing as if all we had passed through that was terrible beyond language had been stripped to this single, gathering sound and it was our word, our language. And I gathered up the greens in my hands, the peppers burning into the small cuts, burning the tender flesh between fingers and nails, and I stuffed that hotness into the holes I had made, pushing them in deep, deep.

I turned the ham over and repeated this process and then I lay it on the bed of green and wrapped it round and tied it shut with twine, the moaning passing lip to lip, reverberating in tremble of my fingers, working that meat. I put the ham on the rack I'd prepared, in a deep pot of water, and I covered it. I boiled it for hours, sitting cross-legged and motionless, sweating. Then I took it from the fire and I let it cool in its own juice for the rest of that night.

In the morning I drained it and I brought it to Hallam.

The other guards followed me at a small distance, and they stood back when I went inside. Hallam's tentmates were still there. They looked up at me with an animalistic dullness from their starved lethargy, their nostrils twitching at the smell of the meat, their mouths salivating.

"Get out," I said.

They stared at me, or rather at the bundle in my hands, transfixed, and I said the words again. As if they were a signal, my companions poured into the tent, screaming my words like echoes, kicking, beating, driving all the prisoners out. All but Hallam.

He lay as I had seen him before, befouled and stinking, his eyes unfocused. I sat down on the earth next to him.

"Hallam," I said, "do you know me?"

His yellowed eyes rolled back in his head. A brownish liquid dribbled down his chin. I seized his jaw between my thumb and forefinger, a gesture remembered by my very skin: the way he would seize me and search my face each time he would see me. His flesh felt rough and hard on its surface but rotten soft underneath, like wood undermined by termites.

"Hallam," I said.

"Hallam," He echoed hollowly.

I laughed. "Yes, Hallam. I bring you something to eat, Hallam. To give you strength. Here." With my free hand, I tore off a chunk of ham. The juice and stuffing clung stickily to my fingers. I pushed it under his nose.

"This is the flesh of your flesh," I said. "Eat of it."

He gagged, his eyes rolling. His hand came up feebly to hold my wrist, but he shrieked when we touched, his rotted fingers bursting and bleeding at the slight contact, as if something in my skin had burned him.

"Eat," I said.

I squeezed my grip until his mouth opened, the stench from the blackened stubs of his teeth and his rotted gums as strong as death. I pushed the ham and greens into that black gap, mashed it into his mouth like a grotesque second tongue. He gagged and swallowed, his eyes rolling. The pink meat mixed with the bile of his insides, his blood; it all spilled out on my hand. Behind him, the other guards watched us silently, a row of grinning heads.

"Hallam," I thought he tried to say.

"Vomit, Hallam," I said. "Vomit Hallam. Vomit me, Hallam."

I pushed more meat into his mouth. He vomited. As if I were floating above myself, drifting up to the apex of the tent, I saw myself, Hallam before Hallam.

I rose and then I knelt and I picked him up. I cradled him in my arms as if he were my child. The bear of a man I remembered was slight, nothing. As we passed outside, the sunlight touched his panicked face and he buried it in my chest. I felt his lips flutter against my skin, as if my heart were beating outside my body.

He only raised his face when the entrance of the hospital suddenly shadowed us. When he looked up and saw where we were, a great cry issued from his lips.

"Noooo. Hallam. Noooo."

"God of Abraham, save us," I whispered into his ear, but I carried him into the darkness, to the dark gods of the Whydah.

It was two days before I could bring myself to go back to the hospital. He lay on his back on the cot, staring up at the ceiling. A bowl of gruel had been placed next to his head, apparently so he could turn his face and lap it like a dog. But either inadvertently or in order to torment him, it had not been placed quite close enough for him to "reach." The gruel was congealing, untouched. A beetle had drowned in its sticky substance.

He stared at me vacantly when I stood over him. He was shrinking into his death, the flesh melting, the skull emerging. I pulled the tattered blanket from him. His yellow flesh had sucked down to the ladder of bones in his chest. His belly was distended with bloat and bristled with a coarse black fur. Tight between his legs, that purse of life, the cursed sac from which unwanted issue was released into the world, was shriveled and black, void of the appearance of flesh. But his arms, down to the stubs of his wrists, lay smooth and innocent at his sides. They weren't horrors, but seemed simply inhuman, mere sticks. Only the stumps themselves looked badly; the surgeon had cauterized clumsily and the flesh there was cracked with bleeding scabs. As I stared, he raised his two arms and brought them together in a strange fashion: the two wrists almost but not quite touching. It took me a moment before what was in his mind emerged as a picture in my own: he was grasping, as if in prayer to me, what was no longer there to grasp: his phantom hands. A prayer, I thought, for forgiveness, but then I saw that his eyes were fastened to that bowl of rancid gruel.

I looked down at him. His passivity, his cringing focus, his utter non-comprehension, suddenly enraged me. Picking up the bowl of gruel, I flung it across the tent. His cauterized wrists waved in its direction helplessly, like the broken antennae of some gigantic, foul insect. Waved at me, as I fled the ward.

I fled, but that night I came back to him. I took him up in my arms and carried him to the ward door. I waited until the sentry had passed, and I carried him outside. He was so light that when I went out into the darkness, I could imagine my arms empty, as if I were carrying smoke. Sergeant Tanner was on duty that night. I had testified in his behalf at the hearing that had been convened after the Norris shooting, a marker I'd called in, though I believe he would have let me do what I wished to do anyway. He imagined I was taking Hallam to finish him. Brother murderer he thought me, though it was murder of which I wished to be relieved. Tanner made sure that no one stopped me, questioned my burden. My burden was light as smoke in my arms and he was the very weight of my life.

I had hidden the skiff under some brush off the Potomac shore and I thought I saw his eyes widen and grow brighter when he saw the water. He was a Hallam, Chesapeake-born; his blood, like mine, run through with estuarine water, that mixture of sea and fresh, the water from the heart of the continent that flushes out its sediment and flows into and dilutes the salt tears of the ocean Passage. A mix of waters that bears and nourishes its own strange, tearing bits of life, species that could not live in the unmixed, pure essence.

I rowed until the shore was a gray seam against the sky, then set the sail. A fog drew around us, and water and sky and time coalesced until I didn't know if we were floating or flying, Hallam and handless Hallam, in a gray ether in which there was only the rasping of his breath, mingling with the groan of canvas, the whistle of wind. If the wind held it would not take me long to get to the other side, and if my luck held as well, I could avoid the Secesh patrols. I knew these waters; I'd fished them for this man's dinner, helped crab and oyster them for my mother's pot. It was a long, wild shore on the Virginia side; I'd leave him on it, one of their patrols would find him. That was my plan. That would have been my plan if I had one, but in truth there was no plan to my voyage, no *logos*, but only a pure and wordless animal need for the relief of weight.

I felt the tick of my heart beat in my palm against the tiller, like an inexorable measure of time. My hands, my skin, my ears all told me I was heading in the right direction, but for all I knew I could have been floating in a fantastical bubble towards the moon. Hallam lay against the bow of the skiff. He raised his face and looked at me through the mist, his face and form, hands gone, wrists wrapped with a breath of smoke, dissolving into that pale opalescent grayness. He smiled. He was fifteen feet from me, at the other end of the boat, but I could feel that smile print like an icy kiss on my lips. He smiled and then he cackled and rolled over the gunnel. I raced to the side and looked over, but all I could see were those two flayed stumps breaking through the mist, their phantom grip squeezing my heart. Then he was gone and I could feel him sinking, sinking, his weight growing heavier inside me as he settled deep.

It was shortly after Hallam's escape that I was transferred from the prison: not because of any suspicion accruing to me from Hallam's disappearance (Tanner had covered me well) but rather because my constant petitions were at last answered. So it was I finally came to the war. And while I was late to the fighting, I saw enough to relegate my memory of Hallam's last days to a small horror, only a comparative (I wanted to believe) by which to measure other horrors. I have seen paralyzed men constantly pinch and prod the flesh of their deadened limbs as if they had to endlessly demonstrate the lack of feeling to themselves. Hallam's pain and death became a vision I touched in just such a manner: only (I told myself) as a test of my numbness. I became, as all good soldiers do, a strange construct without heart or voice, designed only to advance, to aim, to shoot. A pair of feet, a pair of eyes, a pair of hands.

I returned only this far into Southern Maryland: when Father Abraham was murdered by that popinjay of an actor, I was among the troops who hunted him down into Charles County, who followed him over the Potomac. I watched him burn in that Virginia barn, but I felt nothing, neither pity nor delight. All of the fires inside me had already turned to ash.

Afterwards, I rode off by myself, as if to make official the desertion I had taken from my own soul, from lux, years before. I rode north along the river. It was still dangerous country for a black man, particularly one in a blue uniform, but the few whites I saw, furtive and emaciated, looked at me and looked away, afraid of whatever they saw in my eyes, as surely as they feared the rifle slung from my saddle.

I rode until my stomach growled with hunger, and then, as if pulled to the water, I stopped before a dock with most of its planking torn off, but with a skeleton of boards connecting the pilings that marched out into the river.

The dock was off a small meadow; as I rode down to it, I passed the bloated corpse of a cow. I stopped and dismounted. My horse calmly nibbled on the grass near it; like me, he had grown indifferent to carrion. With my bayonet, I sliced off a chunk of the maggoty meat, then cut that into small pieces. The slicing motion of my blade reminded me, for the first time in many months, of the way I had prepared a meal for Hallam. I took a coil of cord from my saddle bag and I fastened the rancid hunks of meat every two feet along the line, using the trot-lining knot Hallam had taught me when I was a small boy, the string looped over itself, each loop tightened like a small noose on the meat. Then I made my way over the framework of boards to the end of the dock, and sat on the small remaining platform of cross boards between the last two pilings. Sat out over that water.

I tied the cord to a piling and threw the end into the river, then I took the slack in my hand, holding it lightly between thumb and forefinger. I had no net or bucket: inasmuch as I thought at all, I thought to pull the crabs out, one by one, and bayonet them. I sat for a long time, dangling my feet, the water flowing around me and from me in a silver stillness. The river pulled the line, as if testing what it had on the other end. Soon I felt the smooth cord begin to tug and jerk harder against my skin, as if it had taken into itself the essence of the life feeding at it, the claws grabbing at the chunks of offal. I began pulling the line slowly in to me, gently so as not to startle the feeding crabs, feeling their slight back tug, the tug between hunger and fear on which we are all strung. Soon I could see one, then two dark shapes growing under the silvery skin of the water, their appendages moving at me like frantic fingers as they broke through the surface.

AMERICAN GRASS

I OPEN MY EYES. The old man, I realize, is pinching me. Crab scurries over my thighs and boobs. Let him; I've paid more for rides. *Chao ong,* he says to me, almost under his breath, like leaving out a little piece of bait. Little wire pig bristles of hair clumped inside his ears. Shirt buttoned up to his neck wattles. Me looking at him thinking the same thing he's probably thinking looking at me. *They're everywhere.*

I turn from him and let my forehead tap tap into the cool glass, watching what flows by the window. *Ma,* the word for ghost drifts into my mind and I play with that, play with being Ma, her wandering soul blown into me. My own lost Mama Ma, a restless VC ghost, blown over here to the World. Loose in the enemy capital. I can see the big white dome now just like the pictures. We drive around it and down a wide street. He slows down, the car, not his hands, his eyes half closed and I see a street sign, the one I've been looking for. I finger walk my own hand over to his crotch, the inky, dinky spider...grab and twist. He screams and slams on the brakes and I'm out the door and gone, running out of a shit storm of horns and brakes and screams. Thanks for the lift. Exit Kiet. *Chao ong,* mother fucker.

After a minute I force myself to slow down and walk calmly down along the sidewalk, trying to look part of it all, a fish in the water of the people. Just like Ma would have done. I flow with the tourists, seeing some vets among then now, wearing their ribbons and buttons and wheelchairs, some of them bony and eaten away, their faces like sticks chewed on the inside by insects, hollowed and caving in, others bulging and oozing out of the gaps between the straining buttons on their old fatigues like that's all they got to hold them from melting off into nothing. All of them turning and staring at me in my black clothes and sandals and VC eyes. Then I see that all the vendor trucks along the street are manned by VC homies too, selling hot dogs and egg rolls and copper Washington Monuments and Sno-Globes, (turn them over and shake them and napalm falls on a thatched roof village), and t-shirts saying *tough shit yeah we're here now,* their Vietnam faces squinting at me like who's this dust? The kind of cool I want to learn someday, learn how to look through people like they're the air behind themselves. Down I go, past them, past the white, columned buildings, down alongside the long pool. Seeing myself a black spoiling speck against all that gleaming white. This skinny VC on the run, weeks in the jungle on nothing but a handful of moldy rice and stinky fish and burning hate. The last and furthest point of the 1990 Tet offensive.

I see the Word in front of me on a sign, like it had leapt out of my head. Word for a place so angry and stubborn it means the same as a war. I follow the sidewalk down and there it is.

And here I am.

I walk closer. On the grass is a bamboo cage, under a sign: *AMERICANS ARE STILL HELD CAPTIVE BY ASIA: POW'S NEVER HAVE A NICE DAY.* Inside, a man in a tattered, tiger stripe flight suit, looks at my face, my black clothing and frowns. His leg is manacled. Nearby, people are clustered in front of the little stands that hold the name books. I know what they are. I know where I am. The sidewalk slants down in front of me to the two wings of the black granite Wall, like they're the open pages of a book themselves. I wait in line. The books are under like the plastic they have over salad bars in restaurants, so you can touch but you can't breathe on it or put your face down into it or kiss it or lick it or bite it. 58,108 listed, a woman in a pink mumu dress says, shaking her head. Like she's going to say, whoo-ee. I put my hands into the slot under the scratched plastic and turn the pages, skimming the lists of names ranks and towns and dates and numbers of panels and lines. Like 15E 33. Like a phone book of the dead. What would happen, I go to a phone, try that number? Who'd answer? Not that I know my dad's name. The name they gave me was just something issued. GI Government issue. I look it up anyway. It isn't there. I look at my face, the enemy's face, floating transparent over the names. GF: Ghost Face. GI: Ghost Issue.

I close the book and start walking down to the Wall. I'm sharp with hunger and clear the way I get sometimes on the street. On my right, I see the three bronze soldiers, one of them my black daddy, looking in astonishment at me, here. I look away, over at the names. But I can't go down to them. Like they being finally touchable real would take them away from me forever.

Three girls are staring at me, giggling, eating egg rolls. Lunch with the dead. Three mall rats in their yuppie kid baggy khaki, like the lost expedition of rich bitches. Maybe my age. Two tall blonds and another gook like me, only shorter, squatter; they keep her for amusement. Only now they got me. Wrinkling their noses, looking at my face, my black clothes, this off-brand grrrl ghost. Roll their eyes, whisper. Laughter dribbles, they press it back inside, swallow it.

Me, I'm hungry.

I'm the Tet offensive, I say to blond one.

Excuse me?

She's astonished to be addressed by dust.

No.

What is your problem? blond two says.

She thinks I'm a rock group.

You numbah hucken ten.

What are you talking about? The dwarf glares at me, their funny face doll, their dusty pet.

She thinks I'm just offensive.

She no speakee, speakee, blond one says. It's the funniest thing they ever heard, so she says it again.

I'm no seey-seey, I say. You can't see me. I live in tunnels under your stupid fucking lives.

I snatch blond one's egg roll and begin eating quickly. Hey, she yells. I see a park ranger, Smokey the Bear hat and all, walking towards us. I start to move. Hey, the dwarf yells, she doesn't want to be left out, and throws her egg roll at me. It explodes, a warm burst heart, tiny shrimps and slimy cabbage on my chest. The VC live off the land, Ma tells me. Bonus. I grab it as it slides and off I go.

Ma N Kiet on the run.

No Lie.

I find a little jungly screen of bushes and sit there, eating the burst eggroll and watching the flow of the river until it gets dark. The water crinkles and sparkles in the last light of the sun, and then, so slowly I can't remember when it happens, the color is sucked away and there's only a heavy sliding blackness in front of me, erasing everything, carrying it all away, a scum of moonlight oily and slick on it. A boat goes by, outlined in lights, people eating, dancing on its deck. Music drifts to me. I squint and try to see another boat behind it, people shitting over the side, hanging onto each other, glued together with their own sweat and stink. *Hey! Wait for us.*

I pat my shirt pocket, making sure what's left of the other egg roll is still there. A horse whinnies, like this crazy laugh. I hear the clatter of hooves coming closer and then I remember that the cops here sometimes ride horses. I scoot back under the overhang of the bush. Someone has used this nest before, left crumpled cans, a wrinkled, twisted condom hanging on a twig, its little bulb still heavy and swaying. The horse passes so close by I can see its breath push at the lace of leaves and branches over my face, feel the thud of its hooves stomping down near my head. I roll out, scramble to my feet and run, zig-zagging into the dark, the horse rearing up in the corner of my eye. I hear the cop shout. I lay down, black on black, and he gallops by me like a movie. Laying there, I think for a while, motionless, and then I know where to go. Where I knew I was going to go anyway, chased by the US fucking cavalry or not.

Only a few people are there at this time of night, passing like shadows in front of the names, some of them squatting in front of the panels. The MIA cage is empty. I slip in between the bars, slip on the leg manacle, lay down on my back and try to look like a pile of rags. Or like part of the exhibit. I'm home.

I take the egg roll out of my shirt, nibble on it a little to calm myself, then put it down. Someone goes by, looks in at me, catches his breath, moves on. Out of the corner of my eye I can see the Wall. The names faint lines in the moonlight, scratches on a dark mirror. Shadows move along in front of them, touching and patting them with pale hands. I draw my knees up and put my face down against them and try not to think. Then try to think about other things. Try not to think about the Wall. The Wall on the Mall. I think about taking Ma shopping, to a real Mall. Like the one I hung at a few days, where the old man picked me up? Showing that to Ma. How would she see all that concrete and glass? Like a scaly dragon lying in the sun? A mouth door that hisses open as we come near. A cool gray gullet that swallows us. Looking up at the squares of mirrors in the ceiling, seeing my long black hair, my slitted eyes, my black clothing. *Attention, shoppers, there's a VC loose in the Mall.* Cold dead air touches Ma's cold dead skin. *Eat,* a sign tells us. You bet. Check out all these choices, Ma. What'll it be? *Wok N Eggroll, Steak N Fries, Bagels R Us, TCBY. This Can't Be You.* Hard light shines through Ma's wavy form reflected in the display windows. Welcome to the World, Ma. Which World? *Mattress World. Video Empire. Computer Universe. Ghosts R Us.* People staring at the mannequins dressed like dreams of the mannequins and in front of one window they're staring at a woman who's pretending to be a mannequin, crying out with mean delight if they can get her to make human movements and I want to kill them all, waste them all. *Fifteen Year Old Viet Vet Ghost Runs Amok. Possessed by VC Soul, Claims Deranged Teen.* Ma gliding cool as can be past stacked rows of TV screens in a window, a blackpajamaed form flowing screen to screen and I turn to try and catch her but she's gone, with only my funny, mixed-up, nothing face there, Kiet-Keisha's dust face staring back at me from screen after screen.

Someone pinches me.

I'm at the Wall.

In front of me a skinny white man with thin patchy red hair. Only where he lost it on his head, it grows like fox fur on his arms and cheeks. This I see plainly, in the light from sidewalk and street lamps, the moon. Hair so red and thin it makes the white scalp under it whiter, like bone. Eyes gleaming. Bony face smudged with dirt, camouflage fatigues stiff and stinking. Bony white hand reaching through the bars of the cage. Only not a hand. One of those metal claw thingies they give you instead of hands. The two pincers covered in black and he's attached little chicken bones on the material. Cool. I hope they're chicken bones.

Hey, little gook, he says, that's my gig.

Just Homeless, I think as I unshackle and scramble out, quickly, still shuddering. He goes in, sits down and slips on the leg manacle. Both hands, I see, are the same. I reach back in through the bars. He slaps my hand. The metal and bone hurts.

I left my egg roll, I say.

He picks it up, sniffs it, looks me up and down, recognizing me. You hungry, Mizzus Cong? he says. Hungry for the food of the East. Hey kid—want an egg roll?

He puts his claw between the bars, snatches it back when I reach. Be polite, Mizz Charlie. Bites off half, pushes the rest through the bars, watches me. Beats out a rhythm with his rattley claws.

Mizz Charles
sucking on mah egg roll
sucking on mah brain box

asken for a bagel lox
asken for a chop stick
asken for a sweet n sour
asken for another hour...

So what they call you, Mizz Charles? he asks.

Nothing.

Yeah? Me too. Used to be Skip. I come from this place, see, everybody called Skip, Buzz, Chip, right? Like noises. Like nothing. So now I'm just Missing. Oozed out between the names. The space between the lines. Like this little red toadstool, right? Pops out, swells up, grows. This polyp. So come on. What's your name?

Lucy, I say, lie. No way I'll name my soul to this one.

Juicy Lucy? So you're here too, huh Luce? Came on over. Followed me back. So how do you like the World? Gotta be better than that shithole, right? Hey, you know something, Lucy? Know what I heard? From the odd wandering monk or two? All that country over there that was scarred up, destroyed by orangeaid and napalm and stuff—it's all growing out again. Only instead of jungle or bamboo or good paddyland, it's all coming up in grass. Tough grass. The gook farmers hate it. They can't weed it—too deep rooted, the roots tangle up under the ground, strangle other plants. They call it American grass, Mizz Charles. It grows everywhere. At night it comes into the villages, creeps up the walls of thatched hootches, penetrates, makes strange changes. It creeps into the bodily orifices of sleeping farmers and their wives. Morning comes, they wake up with this urge to develop, buy stuff, name their kid Lucy.

They love Lucy, I say.

How you know that show? How old you, fifteen, sixteen? You don't remember nothing, do you? Got no idea. Got on the boat, got off the boat. Got welcomed with open arms. Meanwhile, me, I never got back. I'm missing. I never had a parade. Nary a muster. The thing was I was afraid to come back, see, because I heard about all those spitters, right? I heard there were spitters everywhere. Gobbers, hawkers, oyster spewers

97

waiting for me at airports, train stations, Greyhound bus terminals, ferries, ox cart junctions, any public transportation whatsoever. Even at home. Town mayor, county commissioners, cops, even Ma, Pa, granny, little sis, dog, the whole extended family coming out to hawk one on me. Figured wherever I went, let me tell you Lucy, things would get wet and drippy. Screw that. Better to stay missing. People'd treat me just like I was a gook. Like I developed these epicanthic folds, see?

He pulls his eyes narrow with the two tips of the claws. Me, you, same-same, right?

No way. Not me. I'm Vietnam grass, man. You touch me and I'm coming in, right through your pores, your asshole. I'll come in while you're sleeping and I'll fill your throat, my little tendrils wrap around your voice box so you can't scream. My roots'll push into your lungs and stomach, under your skin, wrap around your guts, inside your eyeballs, your balls—you try and pull them out and you'll pull out your insides, man, your heart.

He stares at me. You're the love of my life, he says. No shit. Hey, Juicy Charley, don't worry; I could be your daddy, right?

You ain't nobody's daddy. Get out of my head, man. You can't do that, go in pull shit out of people's heads.

He grins, scratching his chest with his bony pincers, digging into the skin. You met your real daddy, what you do?

Fuck a whole buncha daddies.

He throws back his head and laughs. Like a stream of clicks pouring out of his mouth, like there's a mass of crickets bulging in his throat. Don't say nothing else funny, I tell myself.

How bout your mama? You remember her?

Ma means ghost, you know that? I ask.

Tip of the ectoplasmic iceberg, Luce. You guys got all kinds a ghosts, good and bad. But the bad ones—oo-ee, Lu-cy. Wandering spirits; people killed with violence, with the old extreeeme prejudice, who never had altars built for them. Listen, I know; I got one a them too. No shit. You know the name of mine? Willy Peter. That's White Phosphorous to all you civilian Fucking New Guy Charlies. Willy's this white luminous cloud, all the little particles bury themselves in your flesh, burn like hell, melt the flesh right off the bones. Cover him with mud and the burning stops. But the minute the mud dries, cracks, air gets in—he's back. Burning right down to the bone. Like memory. Know what I mean, kiddo? Get air on it, it *burns*, baby, burns baad. Old Willy Peter. He waves at the Wall. But you guys are smart, see, you build altars for those wandering spirits. Like a shelf, they can come rest. Like a Wall they can hang on to. You gotta build them an altar, so they won't wander around, fuck with the living. Come once a year, light some joss sticks, say their names. Say, hi guys, how's it hanging? Show em you care. Give em an egg roll. You think any of this is an accident, Miz Charlie? It's like it came after us. Like you did. Since when Americans build altars for wandering souls, come here, talk to em, leave offerings? Flowers, wreaths, photos, cigarettes, teddy bears. Just like the altars over there where they died. Just like you come here, kiddo. Like you want to rest, come in, stay with us for a while, little guy...

I run. From his claws reaching out through the bars. From the part of me that wants to seep back in through the bars like a tendril, curl up, stay right there with him in the cage.

I run down into the black V, his cricket laughter clicking louder and louder behind me. The black Wall folds around me. I go down, down, in, in, the Wall growing taller and taller. The moonlight is bright and I can see my reflection flowing wavy around the white shocks of the names. The names give little tugs and pinches at my insides. Spider scurries. My Ma's name is my face reflected in the polished stone. My daddy writes his name on my forehead but whenever I try to see it another name nudges it and replaces it. A murmur follows me, the names clucking in disapproval. I lean my forehead against the cool stone, the names are stitching themselves to my forehead, licking me like stupid fucking puppies, take me home, take me home. I push my whole body against the wall. Daddy daddy daddy daddy daddy 58,108 times. A cloud covers the moon and I disappear into the black Wall. Black into black. I push like I'm pushing into the cold skin

WRITING AFTER WAR

Tuesday, November 6, 1990

Alex—

    I'm sitting here in the dark, the orange letters on the screen
the only illumination in the room. I've come to enjoy writing
like this, as if I'm sitting in my own mind. Outside the darkness
is seemingly absolute, though as I glance through the window,
beyond the transparent, orange tinged reflection of my face
pasted on it, my eyes tease out a flitting shadow, black against
black, or perhaps a current of deeper black within black, and I
think of my runaway girl. Or an emissary, a shadow thought
from you, naked mind to naked mind. You—your body—is only
a few yards away, really, in your studio in the barn. I touch this
keyboard and try to feel in my fingertips what your fingers feel.
The clay cool and smooth and elusive as darkness. I'll write this
and toss it into the ocean of whatever silence lays between us.
My friend Beatrice, the Grief Counselor (I can see the twist of
your lips as I type these words. *Grief counselor. Good grief.*),
recommends that her hospice clients write to their own sense of
loss as a form of coping with grief. That seems appropriate to
me. In the situation we find ourselves in, Alex. Grief. Loss. Write
a letter to it, the Grief Counselor says. Get it out. Turn it into
words that can fly off your heart. Maybe write *"free"* on the upper
right corner of the envelope, the way you would when you sent
me letters from the war. So I take her advice. Why not—I'm a
counselor too; Alex, I lead a useful life built on assumptions of
fixability. And what a comfort in the night that must be, you

told me once. As if you're bound to spend the rest of your mortal time trying to prove false the notion that the human heart can be soothed.

Did I ever tell you my idea of Hell? Hell, my Alex, is a perpetual university seminar filled with Earnest Seekers from our generation, miners for hearts of gold all stuck forever in a close room lit by buzzing neon tubes and heated by sweating pipes. All in our places with bright shiny faces. The windows all steamed up. A seminar with one of those awful titles, like *Connecting with Your Vet,* or *Writing After War.* Hell is a party at the end of the war. Remember? Fifteen years ago, Alex. We'd been invited by one of my professors at American University, that woman who felt my marriage to you made me interesting. The Shrinks and Academics had just discovered the Vets. Remember? Fifteen years before the ships began gathering in the Gulf. And the North Vietnamese army was moving into Saigon, on the television over the wet bar. A tank with a red star on it breaking down a gate. The party-goers cheered. But you cheered the loudest. Remember? You began toasting dead men, shouting out their names and the places and manners in which they'd died. You were past the fifteenth when the room became silent. And we are more than happy to share this moment with you, you said, smiling at them. All of us.

Alex, you did share it with us. All of us. *Free.* It's everywhere. It's leaked into the matrix. Alex, we get it. In Vermont, a man holding an M-16 broke into a loan office, took hostages, set up booby traps, then fought the police in what he described, when finally captured, as a Vietnam flashback. Only he had never been in the war, was far too young. Yet the psychologists who examined him were convinced that he really believed he had been. The lines have been blurred. Massive Seepage has occurred. We are all at the party. We're all in our places with vacant, dull faces.

But I'll lay you have some problems with that, don't you? With the whole seepage thing. Good grief, you'd say. More like the incontinence thing, you'd say. I can hear you. But then—

what's Kiet to you? Answer me that, buddy? And while we're at it, let me tell you about a man and a woman I saw at our hospice group. (What a concept, you said, when I told you I was volunteering to work at the hospice. A place you go and wait around to die. Seems redundant, you said: what place isn't? Alex, sometimes I could plow your face into the ground. Sometimes I could frag you). The man was named Diaz—long, black Indian hair and a sharp-edged hustler's profile, cheeks pitted and raked, clawed by some hard history. But all of it, the whole outlaw look, was like a representation of what he once was. Or a memorial to it. Do you know what I mean? That wasted brittle look that means they're barely attached now. Bone, a hank of hair, a brilliant last spark of brightness in the eyes. The woman—her name was Helen—was wearing what seemed to be a Chinese quilted coat with a matching purple turban wrapped around her head. A few strands of straw-brittle hair stuck out. Her cheeks were caked unevenly with a fleshy pink powder; the skin that showed through was white as bone, like death peeking through the flesh. She must have been about my age. The man, Diaz, had long, beautiful fingers, spots of bright red in the webbing between them, like permanent punctures, misplaced stigmata. Jailhouse tattoos. They were both supposed to be writing narratives, dealing with their anger and grief through imaginative journeys. Not letters but stories. Make up a character, put him/her on a journey, see what happened. What a concept. But Alex, they both wrote about the war. Diaz read me the one he'd written. His character, the Hispanic Warrior, wanders the country after he returns, trying to rediscover America, helping exploited Native Americans and other minority groups. The Hispanic Warrior's time in the Nam has sensitized him to the pain of others. When were you there, I asked him. No, man, he said, I never been anywhere, except jail. Jail's my Nam, man. AIDs my Nam. He looked at me in sly triumph, a con conning. Can I read now, Helen asked me. Her war story. Young Staff Sergeant Lance Harding arrives at a fire base, meets his CO and First Sergeant. Wises off and gets and destroy missions going after the enemy missed by chemicals and radiation, after the invisible guerrilla that has infiltrated and subverted and undermined the soft weight of organs, the marrow of the bone.

HOME

ONCE UPON A TIME, I'd tied up with this guy named Tran who saw me on the street, started talking gook to me. He'd thought it was a put-down when I couldn't answer. When he found out what I was, he laughed and said Kiet-Keisha, girl, in Vietnam they call kids like you dust, dirt like us, bay-bee we were born to blow. He was sixteen, a year older than me, but his parents were alive and both Vietnamese, they'd come on the Hard ship a story of determination and courage you'll never forget on NBC at nine. Had a sister in the Air Force Academy, getting honors in Napalm or some shit and a brother in premed and his parents had a similar model minority part in mind for him too. So he stole his parents' dream machine and drove right out of the movie of the week. He liked cars about as much as he liked to teach me cars. Gave me the gift of move. The two of us doing doughnuts at midnight in a hot-wired 88 Taurus when the cops got him and I got away. One other thing he taught me though, you're out in Neck country and you really want wheels to go someplace instead of just joyriding around, you pick something that fits in. The kind the owner might take their time calling the cops or might not be a cop-calling sort of person at all. Something scrungy like this truck. Dented up roof, scraped paint, beer cans crumpled on the floor, stuffing poking out of the seat, roaches in the ashtray, sticker: *My Kid Beat Up Your Honor Student.*

I pass one police car, he doesn't even look at me down here. This truck right at home here. Knows where it's going.

I know where I'm going. Touched one daddy and pushed off the Black Wall like the side of a pool and now I'm swimming back towards the other. Point Lookout. The point from which I'd started my run, booked, left the Program. VC slick, right; who'd think of looking for me there? Going home. Seen one dad, now going to see the other. Going to see my foster pervert. Me and Ma. *Get some*, old bony-handed Willy Peter had said. Lookout, lookout, lookout, dads, coming for you. Little pissed-off wandering soul, snagged out of the slide of water and time, going down and down to it, into the boonies and among the angry ghosts again.

Thinking all this, like being a ghost can protect me from the real ghosts. From the *tinh* who could reach into my open mouth and pull out my soul and leave me husked and drooling and empty. The *tinh* that had been chasing me all my life and he would never let me go, not to my last breath. And there aren't many streetlights now, or for that matter many houses either along the side of the road. Just a dark wall of pine trees, the moon overhead, too bright with none of its light stolen into neon signs. A few cars pass me, but there's not much traffic. I'm back. I turn off on a small road and stop the truck on the shoulder. The moonlight follows the road down a hill, through thick dark woods. I see the lights of a few houses, just enough to give me the shape of the road. I get out and walk down the road, close to the side, ready to disappear into the woods. I walk in the shadows. I creep and crawl. I peek in windows.

But all the houses on the street are sealed and peopled. No empties. All I get is a barn. Only it's not like an animal barn. This picture I have of lying up to some warm cow, sheep. But nothing there but tobacco hanging from the ceiling like dead alien fingers, dry and scratchy. Rustling and cackling all night all around me. Nicotine fit.

Morning I stick to the woods, trying to scope out more houses, find one with no car or truck in the driveway, no activity. No luck. Except the garbage pails behind one, I score nearly half a Big Mac, some fries, little packets of ketchup. I stay easy all day, find a nest in some bushes, lie back, look at the sky.

By dark I start moving again. I get back to the road where I left the truck. It's gone. I'm cold. I need an empty place. A place I can drift into. Dust seeping into the secret wounds only I can see in houses.

I slide up to the first house, look into the window. A man and woman in all their glory, doing it. I watch for a while, feeling the power of my situation. I'm invisible, I can reach right through the window and touch them, they'd only feel a shiver on their skins. Some part of them knowing I'm the kid they're making, waiting out here, floating.

Look out, look out, look out.

I creep to the second house.

Inside the bright rectangle of a window a TV family, man, woman, two children sit in front of the rectangle of the tube. I watch with them, floating invisible behind their shoulders with just the thin glass between us so it's like I'm watching them on TV watching another family on TV. Outside all these lives. So cold out here, I'll moan, smiling at the children from the dark outside their window, hoping they will turn and meet my terrible eyes. Hey.

I float on. At the next house on the street I peek into a window and a man is picking up a small boy and flinging him like a sack. He's smiling and the boy is smiling, but the smiles are like masks they are both trying to keep on and I flashback my foster pervert smiling like that and how I'd watch hands knot up into fists, like there was some connecting muscle from that smile to those fists. To his fingers. Mouth hand coordination. Watchoo looking at, ya little gook fuck? Wanna see it closer? Wanna see it probe and stir and gouge.

Co, co, motherfucker, I whisper to the man. Then I get out of there.

I start to go to the house where I saw the couple. But when I look in the window I see the man looking out. Staring right into my face. Squinting like he's looking into a mirror. I run, melt into the woods.

For a while I feel like I'm lost. The trees grabbing me, turning me in circles. Tripping me. Finally though I break through and into a little clearing. Like a bowl of moonlight. In the middle is this little shack, deep in the woods, perfect; what I'm hoping is this is some hunter's place, nice and empty. No windows in front. I try the door. It opens. But when I look inside there's an old black man sitting on a sofa. Black like half of me. Old like I'm young. Eyes, blank as screens themselves, staring at the TV. Blank and crawling with shadows. What's this blind man's doing, watching TV? The one room has gray, streaky plank walls. A little kitchen area, scarred wooden table and chairs, the sofa. A kerosene heater, its grate glowing. Everything neat, with a oval blue rug exactly in the middle of the swept wooden floor, like a center holding it together. No mess. Mess probably be hard for a blind man. On the counter are a couple slices toast. I sneak up, noiseless and smooth as dust, palm them, scoop them into my shirt. Then I wave my hands in front of his face.

I always wonder why people feel they have to fan the blind, he says.

I laugh, I can't help it.

Hey, man, I say, what you watching, that TV?

Reruns, he says.

I bite my lip, liking him, figuring, why not, no way he can see it.

He turns his face to me, eyes socketed with shadow, black on his brown spotted skin, like his blindness has spilled out. His blank stare eating into my skin. To the bone.

Like you, he says.

Reruns. I close my eyes. See clawed fingers fumbling, moving over the sheets. Probing.

I ask, So what you see, you hear me talking?

A red cloud spreading like a dream around green rice stalks, he says. A child, crawling from that water, come to me.

Words like cords he's netting around my mind, shaking it towards him.

You my daddy?

Why not?

His words pouring into my heart like sweet heavy blood, what is happening sliding over what I wanted to happen for so long. Wanting it so bad.

You can stay here, Kiet, he says.

Whoa.

It's no mystery that I know your name, child, he says, as if he reads my mind. People are looking for you. Don't be scared.

I'm not scared. He's not the *tinh*, not him, and if he ain't my daddy, he'll do. That's what I think. And I want bad to stay, this neat place, everything in order and waiting for me. I reach over, almost touch his eyes, the shadows of my fingers sliding across his sockets.

Fuck a whole buncha daddies, I say.

Then I book.

I run through the woods. Run against everything in me pulling me back to that shack. Like to the cage at the wall.

Run right onto a road and nearly get run over by a pickup truck. Some kid in it screams at me out the window, throws a beer bottle at me, like he thinks I'm an honor student. I pick it up, but there's only a little left when I suck on it. I see I'm in front of a house has no lights on.

But two cars in the driveway. I circle around to the back. There's a barn behind the house and light shines from between its boards and falls across the lawn. I avoid the stripes of light on the black ground and go up to the rear of the house. One window has a very small kind of orange light coming from it. I peek inside. A woman is sitting at a desk, her face dark but written on by the orange glowing letters sliding across a computer screen, her fingers tapping messages at a keyboard. A shock rolls through me because this is, no shit, my counselor from the

Home. I feel a chill of fear, like she's written me on her disk and now she's called me back. Save Kiet. I leave the window and go back to the barn. The light's still leaking from it but I still need to check it out, maybe it's empty. I press my face against the openings between the boards. Around the room are forms covered with white cloths. Misshapen clay heads. Work tables. Cans of clay. A man is sitting, turned from me, his back hunched. His hands are working at a tall form in front of him. Its back, to me, is draped. He's pulled the sheet up on his side. On the wall next to him, framed in a photograph, I can see him hunched the same way he is now but over a machine gun, hanging out from the door of a helicopter. Like the ancestors' pictures in Minh's house, but as if he's his own ancestor. His hands on the machine gun then as they are on the clay now. Below him, a straw-roofed village. His face twisted. Demon's face. He slaps water onto the clay, kneads and pinches. He turns to me for a second. His face is angry and terrible. The same face twice, in the picture and aged in the flesh. He makes a fist, slams it on the table, then covers the clay with the white cloth. I see the form bleed through the fibers. His fingers claw at the air. The *tinh* sits staring at his hands as if he wants them to speak. Where is she? he must be asking them, not knowing I'm here, out here.

The *tinh* gets up and leaves the room. I try the bottom of the window. It slides open. I slip inside. On a peg on the wall next to the picture of the helicopter I see a black leather belt with a holster on it. A gun and a badge. I remember him now. White Cop. My counselor's husband, I remember, is a sheriff. But this is a different prison, the secret prison of the *tinh*. I go over to the tall, draped form. But I'm afraid to uncover it.

I pull off the cloth. He's captured Ma's soul and made her perfect for himself. Naked. My height. Slanted eyes like mine. But no mouth to scream. The baby she's holding to her breast is lumpy and rutted. All of its flesh a twisty scar. And she has no nipples to feed it. No belly button to cord it. No sex to give it birth. Blank as a wall. I stand in front of her. I come closer. My shadow moving over her. Smooth pink bumps of breasts. I push against her and take the clay in my mouth, suckle. It's cold and bitter. I reach up and gouge out her mouth and let her scream out. I push in a belly button. My fingers slit a sex. I tear away the baby from her breast and rip and pinch and twist it into pieces. I push my face against Ma's face, push into the cold wet clay. I pick the baby up and throw its torn body through the window. The glass shatters.

A howl of rage. Running footsteps.

I grab the gun and follow the clay baby out through the broken glass and run into the trees. They close around me, whisper and rustle. I go deeper and deeper into them. The moon is big and silver and lights things like a flashlight. *Look here, Kiet.* But I don't. I hear footsteps just behind mine, just behind the curtain of trees. The flesh on my neck shivers like a breath has touched it. I've come to his country and he is hunting me here.

Look out, look out, look out.

Then I'm out of the forest. In front of me is a field full of weeds stiff and silver as an old man's hair under the moonlight. At the other side of it a black square shape against the moonlit sky, a piece cut out of the sky. And I know where I am. And I have a gun in my hand. *Chao ong,* fucker. Dad-dee I'm home.

I run over the frozen weeds to it, breaking their backs. No sound except the high whistling of the wind in the pines around the field and the crunching of my feet. But when I stop a little scurrying noise runs on for a few seconds until it gets lost in the sound of the wind.

I'm near the big darkness of the house now. Something creaks and moans. The front door of the house has been locked up tight. Like he's expecting me. Like dust can't flow through the cracks. But the right window slides up easy when I push it. I slip inside and the moonlight slips in with me and the shadows of the house mix with my shadow so I feel them slide into one another and I move through the house with that soft movement. Dirty snow lumps. I touch one. A sofa, covered with a sheet. A chair. A table. All covered. I check the kitchen. Bare, no furniture, peeling linoleum floor. I open the refrigerator. An old rotty farty smell, empty shelves. Like opening a door to my own cold raw stomach.

Where is he?

The first door on the right opens to a bedroom. No furniture in it but an old-time metal bed, mattress rolled up on it, smelling cold and moldy. No pictures on the wall. No decorations. No rugs. Nothing. I remember a story I read once about humans put in an alien zoo, the cages houses built from the pictures in their minds and hearts. My mind and heart: empty and cold and waiting.

I hear a noise. A shuffling in the hallway. Breathing. I stop and try to untangle the sound from my own breathing. I can't.

I run down the hall, opening doors. All the rooms are empty, the furniture in them is all covered. Finally there's only one door left. My room. I open the door and it's like the aliens took it out of my head. Everything frozen. A curtainless window, the moonlight pouring in brightly. Things he put in and things I put in, still married together. Against one wall my bed, quilts piled on it, a headless Raggedy Ann doll sitting against the headboard. On the wall above it a Berenstain Bear family, a Ninja Turtle poster. Against the other wall is a dresser and above it are shelves lined with Turtle and my old Star Wars and He Man figures: Leonardo and Donatello, Luke and Hans and Leia and Wookie, Skeletor's hooded face giving me its evil little grin. I close the door tightly behind me. I open the closet. Empty. Just the hamper, forgotten clothes still inside.

I hear a scratching from the hallway. A faint shuffling. A creak. Breathing.

Look out, look out, look out.

I open the clothes hamper again. I touch the clothes and towels, reach in, bunch the soft cloth in my hands and plunge my face into them, smelling the leftover sweats and pees and tears, rubbing them into my skin like camouflage.

Then I get on the bed and pile the quilts around me, over me. I hold onto Raggedy Ann. The noise in the hall fades, stops. I peek out of the blankets. Skeletor's mocking face, shadowed by the moonlight, grins at me and I slide my gaze away to the window and Skeletor's face slides with it and as I watch it balloons into the *tinh's* rutted and scarred face framed in the glass. He's staring at me with pure hatred, his eyes black tunnels into the night, his mouth silently screaming curses at me behind the glass of the window and no matter how much I blink, he won't disappear.

THE GOLDEN CHILD

"I HAD A LOUSY DAY, thank you," Louise said, as if Alex had asked her. They were getting ready to go to a Halloween party neither one wanted to attend. Lou's gang, Alex thought. Lou's gang coming home and sitting down with his gang.

"Maybe we should have a contest. I'll trot out my horror stories from work, you trot out yours. Theoretically it should render our private concerns and squabbles trivial."

"You poor dear," she said.

He took a beer out of the refrigerator and sat down.

"What happened?"

"Kiet ran away," Louise said.

Slid right into his evening.

"I thought she was using her American name now. What was it? Keisha? Laquisha? Maharisha?"

Louise laughed flatly. "We decided in group that was identity avoidance."

"Which identity was she avoiding?"

"In Vietnam, kids like her were despised until people found out that American features could get entry visas," Louise said. "Then they were called golden children. Only a lot of them were abandoned when they got here. That's the current wisdom about Kiet. As it were."

Alex shrugged. "I'll put out an alert. Do you know anybody in the community she has contact with?"

"There was a Vietnamese guy—she met him when we stopped to do some shopping at Country Market."

"The Trinhs?"

"No, some guy who was shopping there. Minh something, I think. She got engrossed in a conversation with him. I remember being surprised at her opening up. The Trinhs seemed very quiet around him."

"Youngish, fattish man? Flashy jewelry, beeper?"

"Yes."

Alex nodded. "Minh Van Tran. Guy bought that photo lab, up on Mills Road?" Minh was in his twenties, too well-heeled for someone just came out of a Hong Kong refugee camp last year. Minh, Trinh, he thought. Kiet. What had trailed back after him to his county, to the places of his childhood? Even his new deputy was Vietnamese. "Trung told me he thinks Minh was a gang leader," he said to Louise. "I've wanted to look into him for awhile anyway—I'll stake out his place; she goes in we can get a Town warrant. Look, we'll find her. And you'll get her back. And then what will happen?"

"She'll probably run again. When she's eighteen, we'll let her go. She'll die. You want me to say that? Damn it," she said, as if she'd just remembered something. "She's not there to testify, that son of a bitch Johns will get off, wouldn't he?"

"Probably."

"Do you know why she ran? Brilliant Larry rented tapes for the girls, last night; one was *Platoon*. To the other girls it was boring, the level of violence was too low, they had no historical references. But apparently the village scene—the Vietnamese women the GI's shot?—Kiet made some sort of connection to her mother, maybe to Johns. Next day—she ran."

Alex felt vaguely accused. "Did it happen to her mother that way?"

"She doesn't remember her real mother at all, either of her parents. There's just enough of it out there. The war. She's done this kind of thing before she was fostered to Hiram Johns. We got her after she was picked up at the Vietnam memorial—she'd run away from her foster home in Florida to go there. Someone called the cops—people didn't like the idea of this kid dressed like a VC hanging out there. She goes looking for her father. She clipped a photo of some black serviceman from a newspaper, some our-boys-in-the-service column, and she goes around showing it to people. Sleeping with people."

Alex looked down at his hand, saw he'd crushed the beer can. He had no memory of the act. He tossed the can in the garbage.

"Speaking of photos, here's one of Kiet. So you can post it, whatever," Louise said.

The face looked at him, filled him with anger. "Has she been tested? Or she one of your victims going to go out, make more victims? Spread something."

Louise looked at him. "Alex, what's bothering you?"

"Nothing, counselor. Not a thing. I'd put you right out of fucking business."

Louise was staring at him. He felt as surprised as she looked. He took another beer. His fingers were trembling.

Well, well, he thought.

As he drove past the naval air station, a cargo plane lumbered up into the air, its shadow passing over him. At that moment, a deer leapt in front of his car and bounded across the road, white tail bobbing. It was strange weather for early November—there were snow storms in California while the temperature in Maryland stayed high—and the deer were behaving erratically, as if they felt displaced. Alex sympathized. Over the last months, troop and cargo aircraft had been taking off in migratory flocks from the base to disappear into the Gulf while on the news Americans in sand-colored fatigues were pouring down the rear ramps of the same helicopters they'd had in the war some twenty-odd years ago. Helicopter gunners in flak jackets flashed thumbs-up signs at the camera. Airmen painted funny sayings on their bombs. He remembered how the camouflaged cloth that fit over helmets had two sides, green side out or brown side out; you were given the order according to the season or place. His war had been green side out. Now it was brown side out. It seemed more should change.

A red light blinked suddenly in front of his eyes as if to show him it had. He slammed on the brakes and cursed. The signal was new; so was the shopping plaza to the right of the road that was the reason for its existence. Fox Run Plaza. Next to the new Fox Chase Townhouses. He tried to squint the new stores and the cloistered, store-bordered parking lot back into the shimmer of marsh and forest he remembered here. A few days before there'd been a shooting at the IHOP, and yesterday he'd busted several crack dealers from DC who'd been setting up shop in the scrub pines behind the K-Mart. The dealers, like everyone else, wanted to move to his county.

Below the base the scenery opened up, as if he really had passed a line in time. Fields stubbled with stalks, silver boarded tobacco barns. As Alex looked, the dying light flared and the forest blazed into incandescent reds, a trick of light or memory.

He stopped at Brian Schulman's to ask him if he'd seen any sign of the girl. Schulman, he'd heard, was planning a trip back to Vietnam. Alex didn't have to: at his next stop, the Country Market in St. Inigoes, the Vietnamese couple who owned the store now, the Trinhs, were wearing blue calico aprons and greeted him warmly, smiling, how are you today, Sheriff Alex? Just fine. Where are your young men, what do your smiles mean, what tunnels and traps are hidden under your floors?

He bought steaks, milk, beer, rice, toothpaste and ice cream. He drove into the state park area. A few miles further south, he saw the small no hunting, no trespassing sign that marked the packed dirt and gravel road that went in to Baxter's cottage. The car bumped along its corrugations, under the cool shadows of loblollies, elms, pin oaks. A spot of red flashed in the corner of his eye and as he turned he saw the fox standing, transfixed, near some bushes. He stopped the car. His eyes met the animal's and he felt something quick and wild slide into him. He leaned forward, just a little, trying not to breathe and the fox ran and he felt something of himself run along and disappear. Fox Chase. Fox Run. Fox Die. Staring after the fox, he thought he saw another figure in the shadows. But when he tried to focus on it, it shifted, a bubble brushed by the weight of his attention. He wondered if it were a Point Lookout ghost. Finally seeing one after a lifetime of ghost stories.

He thought of the girl, Kiet, Keisha; maybe she was hiding out near here: the park manager had told him about kids bothering Baxter. Maybe it was the girl. Still in the area. Looking for a home. The golden child. A picture came into his mind, another kind of ghost: Baxter delicately gripping the cyclic control of a helicopter. He pictured Kiet running through the woods, how you shot low and left at a target running on the ground, say if someone panicked because of what she was trying to protect, if someone forgot it was better to freeze.

He turned right again, onto a smaller path. Branches had fallen in several spots and he had to stop to clear brush. No one came here except him, and whatever kids might be harassing Baxter, these days. The land south of Scotland was part of the Point Lookout park, but there were still small houses scattered through the woods, rented out by the state to the families who'd been here when the land was taken over—his own house was on a road just bordering the park, still county land. Baxter had arranged that his disability checks would go straight into an account Alex could tap into; he made sure Baxter's rent was paid to Ed Riordan, the park manager, made sure that Baxter was left alone.

The cottage he'd built for Baxter was the most isolated in the area. Alex saw him sitting, motionless, on the porch now, his black skin a shade of the shadow, the petaled flesh in his ruined eye sockets forming two nestling moths, the scarred skin around them crinkled as bark. Whenever he took him to town, Baxter wore sunglasses. But not at home.

He walked noisily through the dead leaves. A grin split the utter stillness of Baxter's face.

"Ah, Alex. Isn't it early for your visit?"

Did Baxter keep track of the time like a tree? Sounds and smells and shifts in temperature scraping across skin and rooted stillness and memory. "I had reports you've been harassed."

"Only by raccoons."

"Ed Riordan told me he ran some kids off."

"Oh, there's some teenagers, sometimes, especially now around Halloween. I'm one of the Point's ghost stories, a kid's dare."

"My mind, you make a lousy local legend."

"It wasn't," Baxter said, "what I'd envisioned for myself."

The words brought Alex the Baxter he'd known in high school—the county's first integrated class—a yearbook picture of his bright-eyed, earnest face over the kind of caption they'd all had faith contained the directions of their lives like Delphic mutterings: French Club, Student Council, Debate Club, ROTC scholarship. The yearbook still existed in Alex's attic, in a box containing some of Baxter's other books, its covers preserving a world of images—a shimmer of marsh and forest and unseared faces—that for all Alex knew still existed in Baxter's mind.

He got up and brought the food into the kitchen. A moss of dirt covered the table and floor, the screen of the TV Baxter had requested Alex bring him. The inside of the house smelled moldy. He cursed Riordan silently; he'd paid the park manager to get someone in here to clean. He opened the refrigerator and stacked the food inside, thinking about the incongruity of a light in a blind man's refrigerator. Not to mention the television.

"Meat is in the freezer," he called to Baxter. "Beer on the top shelf. Vegetables on the second shelf."

He ran his finger through the staticky fur on the TV screen. When Baxter had asked him for the set, all he could think of to say was: well, hell, then you won't mind black and white. Hell back to you, Baxter had said: all I see anyway are reruns. Alex pulled the on button. A pattern of distorted lines filled the screen. "We bring good things to you," a voice said, and in his mind's eye but vividly, he saw a scramble of images: the Vietnamese couple at the convenience store, the Trinhs; the teasing, leaf-shrouded grin of the figure he'd glimpsed in the woods and then a mollusk-hatted woman reaching her hands down into brown red-stained paddy water and offering up to him a girl baby, a torn child, the silted heavy water bubbling from its mouth. A golden child. He saw Baxter take the child, its hand flapping, its fingers seeming to touch Baxter's face, brushing over his eyes, as if exploring its death, then flopping down. The vision flared and then was gone, a synapse of memory suddenly glowing. A rerun. Only it wasn't a real memory. Not all of it. Don't make it into what it wasn't. There hadn't been a child, only its bulge in the woman's belly, only the woman, solidly real as their rotor wash parted the rice stalks, though he'd shot quickly, automatically, before the details of what she was formed in his eyes, her face, her empty hands. He hadn't thought of the incident in years, not until now. No one had faulted him at the time. Not even himself. If he'd allowed the woman to live and have her child, it would be the same age as Kiet. Though understanding what had brought those particular ghosts, real and never-real, to the surface of his mind now, didn't help. He turned off the set. "Bring back a six-pack," Baxter called to him.

They sat on the porch.

"Thanks, Alex," Baxter said, his hand sweeping the area in front of them, the house, the land.

"How you doing?"

Baxter smiled.

"Mr. Fix-it. You gonna carve off my lonely, Alex?"

"I would if I could."

"I believe you," Baxter said.

Alex opened a beer and drank. He was still a little shaken. "What's your last name?"

"Oh, yes, same as yours. Same as half the other blacks and whites in this county. Same as your black-assed deputy Russell, hates your guts. It don't, as we were wont to say in the late conflict, mean nothing."

Alex remembered suddenly that Baxter, before he'd been wounded and medevacked, had tried to adopt a kid from an orphanage near the base, out in the village where Alex had worked winning hearts and minds before Baxter got him into his crew. At the time he had regarded the gesture, the attempted adoption, as useless and perhaps even hypocritical. But again a picture came into his mind: the child here, whole, silent, her hands touching Baxter's face.

Baxter took his beer can in two hands, moving it back and forth in small circles. Alex watched his hands. The cyclic.

"You think Russell hates my guts?"

"Black Hallams used to have a story—when the Confederate sympathizers in the county were thrown into the POW camp here, you had a black Hallam guard, a Union soldier who tortured and murdered a white Hallam, his old master. Your family have that story?"

"Hell, then I should have the grudge."

"You do."

Alex laughed. They drank the beer.

"What news from the world?" Baxter asked.

"There might be a war."

Baxter coughed again, to show he knew when he was being kidded.

The sky was a hard, spotless blue backdrop against the yellow leaves. The unseasonable warmth had released a locked odor of decay from the earth. Alex closed his eyes and tried to sense it as Baxter would. He felt his skin open under the cold touch of a breeze. There were sounds on the edge of the feeling, soughs and rustles. He thought of the sight that had been scabbed in his own head only to soften and reattach itself to random buzzes and pictures. As if he were a blind man watching TV. What came into his mind now, gashed from one memory to the other, was the stretch of the ditch beneath them on that day, weeks after he'd shot the woman; the soldiers scurrying below

carving the village to that death's head grin impacted with its
masticated, pajamaed dead; the child crawling out of it, as if it
were the child Alex had torn from the world still, inexorably,
pushing towards the light, but grabbed by the heel and flung
back in, as if its birth into the world was disturbing the shape.
He thought of the pilot, what was his name, Thompson? who'd
come down, tried to stop it, had his gunner train his gun on the
soldiers shooting the villagers; he thought, an ache that was so
deep it was almost lust opening in his stomach, of how it would
have been, to descend and intervene, to protect and serve.

"Do you remember how you could see it all from fifteen
hundred feet?" he said. "Every little detail? What do you
remember, Baxter?"

"A white egret on a paddy dike. When the shrapnel hit, I felt
it was the sharpness of that bird's beak, sliding in, scissoring.
That it flew off with my sight. I remember that. And I remember
the green, Alex. The emerald kingdom."

"And we shot the Munchkins."

Baxter turned to him, the scooped out sockets filled with
shadow and reproach. "No, Alex. We just hovered. Hovered and
recovered. Anyway, that was long ago and in another country."

The literary ha'nt, Alex thought. A poet and he knows it.
Minh Trinh Sin.

When he got home, on impulse, he went out to the barn. The
studio—it took up about a quarter of the building's space—was
partitioned off from the rest of the barn by a floor to ceiling
wall. The wall was made of cedar logs, tight-fitting Amish work:
his father had contracted with Johann Schneerson, a horse and
buggy Mennonite who'd owned the land next to theirs when
Alex was a boy, to convert the space. At first, he hadn't been sure
if the studio was a result of his father's pride or came from a
desire to hide away what Alex was doing away: the county hadn't
known how to take a kid like him, old family, football player,

131

county commissioner's son, yet good at art. The equation seemed unbalanced, unnatural. Alex didn't seem queer. That his talent was sculpture, work done with the hands, made it a little more acceptable: whittling ran in the blood people said; the Hallams had built some of the first skipjacks, appropriated the shape of the Piscataway canoe, elongated it, put sails on it, changed it into a design for their own uses. But he was never that good with a knife and wood; it was clay that seemed to come to life in his hands, clay and stone that fell away before his eyes, and then his hands or chisel, to reveal the secret shapes imprisoned within. At eighteen he'd been good enough to win a full scholarship to Pratt: by then he had a room full of figures in the studio, a population he'd brought forth from some mysterious kingdom in his heart.

At night, pretending to sleep, he would sometimes watch his father creep across the patch of ground to the barn, disappear inside, emerge an hour or more later with a secret smile on his face. When he was in the war, he would picture his father going into the building, touching the faces and forms his son had left behind. But when Alex returned, he found that his father had padlocked the door and never went in; he told Alex later that if he hadn't come home, if Alex were killed in Vietnam, he was going to burn the barn down. It was as if he felt the sculptures had called into the world spirits strong enough to protect his son, helpless enough to be threatened with fire.

The pieces he had done then were draped now, the sheets over them stiff with filth or bulged as if they covered the dead. It was cold in the room, a thick undisturbed coldness heightened by the sad wasted smell of undrained gasoline, the smell of neglect.

A blank eye from a half-formed face regarded him balefully from the table in the center of the room, the clay pitted and cracked, a net of supporting wires showing through gaps and tears. Formless lumps pressed in on him with the weight of their incompleteness. Everything was covered with dust. He hadn't been in here for half a year, and the last time he'd tried to work his hands had patted, pulled, kneaded, but the clay had stayed lifeless, stillborn in the layered heaviness of itself. What shapes did start to come out frightened and disgusted him and his hands pressed them back into the gray surface, erased them into a safe blankness.

He thought again about Kiet, the opening of rage in him when Louise brought her up, brought her into his house.

He touched the face, the dryness of the surface. A fine powder gritted his palms. He could still envision the shape waiting for him, the life inside, but as he touched it the life retreated from his fingers, as if an invisible acid were leaking from his pores. His hands felt clumsy, set in a numbing glove between his touch and the world. His hand balled up into a fist, as if he had sculpted it, made it into the only shape he could.

On Monday evening he sat next to Russell Hallam in an unmarked car across the street from Minh's Photo Shop, Hallam and Hallam alone with each other, watching the Vietnamese again. Same as your black-assed deputy Russell, hates your guts, Baxter had said. In the silence now, Alex felt the old tension laying like a waterweight between them, full of dim drowned figures, of crimes of war and family and skin never acknowledged or recompensed. The door opened and he caught the smell of something cooking, a whiff of fish sauce, *nuoc mam*, startling here in the familiar street, something else that had followed him back to this place. A Vietnamese man came out and stood outside the shop door, under the *One Hour Developing/Passport Photos While You Wait* sign. He was smoking a cigarette and looking furtively around like a character in a bad movie. The references were always movies. He thought of Kiet running because she'd seen *Platoon*.

"You ever see *Platoon*?" he asked.

Russell looked disgusted. "'Is that what it was like?' people ask me. Sure. Kill the air conditioning, boobytrap every fifth seat, you'll see what it was like."

The man went back inside the shop.

"Did you see her go in yourself?"

"No. Trung was on stakeout. He thinks the girl answered to Kiet's description. But he claims they all look alike to him. Alex, are you all right?"

Alex looked at the sign. "How do you think the girl would see it? That scene in the village? The murders—killing that woman in the pig sty?"

"Alex, I never shot people like that."

"Lucky you."

"Lucky people."

"The thing is," Alex said, "It was so unreal then, wasn't it? Only now it's gotten real. Like it's been given a shape."

"The thing is, Alex," Russell said, "we've also had calls she's been spotted down to Point Lookout. Some B&E's. The real thing is, Alex, why all this fuss and bother? You put in less time on that killing at IHOP."

"The shooter was arrested."

"The kid will probably come back—they usually do. Why are we going through all this?"

"We're doing it so we have an excuse to check out Minh. Is that a good enough reason for you, Deputy?"

Minh Trinh Sin.

He turned from Russell, picked up the transmitter and radioed to Lavelle. Lavelle's voice boomed back in a roar of static, too loud. Alex twisted the volume down, told him where to deploy the others. Two covering the rear, one in the alley, everybody else in front. They got out and walked to the shop. Alex stood to the side and knocked on the door. No one answered. Alex knocked again. He twisted the knob. The door opened. He heard Russell speak into the radio. "Sheriff's department," Alex yelled and swung inside, crouched, holding his gun in front of him.

Darkness. A sound of something scurrying in it. The rotten egg odor of darkroom chemicals mixed with the smell of rice cooking and *nuoc mam*. He felt a very old fear tighten in his chest and stomach.

"Get the light," he growled to Russell. His voice caught in his dry throat. He heard shouting, his deputies coming in from the other door.

A crash of glass. Trung swearing in the other room. The light flared on, then off like a camera flash. In that moment of illumination he saw a line of Vietnamese, their faces dead white, their eyes socketed in blackness. Mollusk hats, black pajamas. An old woman with a black mouth opened in a scream, hands extended pleadingly towards him. A man pointing an AK-47 at his face, the man's face twisted with hate. Alex fired. Flashes. The smell of cordite mixing with the other smells.

"What the fuck are you doing?" Russell was yelling in his ear. The light came on, stayed on. Russell was staring at him, his hand on the switch. The room was otherwise empty. Shredded paper from the photographs Alex had shot up was still fluttering in the air. One piece, half an old woman's head, landed near his foot. Minh came into the room. He was wearing only baggy boxer shorts, his belly a middle-aged man's belly on a young man, a roll of soft, unhealthy looking flesh hanging over the waistband of his shorts. A woman came after him, tightening the belt on a robe. She looked at the damage Alex had done, then back to him with contempt, exaggerating the look to make sure he got it.

"Everything all right, sheriff?" Trung asked.

"Just fine."

"What do you want?" Minh asked. "Who will pay for this?"

"Minh Van Tran, I have a warrant to search these premises."

Minh's face didn't change. "Why did you shoot my pictures?"

"I shot them instead of shooting your sorry ass."

Minh said nothing.

"Where is she?" Alex demanded. For a second he thought he saw a twitch of panic cross Minh's face. But the mask reformed. He gripped the gun tightly, measuring the arc of its barrel to the center of that blank, staring face.

"Where is she, you son of a bitch?" he said.

"Hey, sheriff," Lavelle called.

Alex walked to his voice, turning quickly, needing to get away from Minh. From M.T. Sin. Empty Sin. The room at the other end of the hallway that he went into was filled with Vietnamese, as if the pictures he'd shot had turned to corporeal form. They squatted or stood, still as photographs, four young men, three young women. None of them was Kiet. The floor was covered with mattresses and blankets. There was a smell of sweat and warmth and sleep and he pictured, envied, the comforting press of flesh here.

One of the men spat at his feet.

"Radio in for some backup," he said to Russell, "and let's get some female deputies for body searches; let's get that done before they leave the room. And better have someone call immigration."

"Ten-four and all other numbers," Russell said.

"Let me see your papers," Alex said in Vietnamese, the phrase rolling out of his mouth as if it had been sleeping behind his tongue. The faces stayed stiff, cold, motionless as the faces he'd seen in the other room, as if a powder had seeped from him, whitened and deadened them. "*Cac ong cac ba,*" he said. "*Toi rat han hanh duoc gap ong.*"

Trung stared at him. "Hey, don't look at me, I'm from Anaheim."

"He escaped from a Disney exhibit, Alex," Russell said. "Little Lt. Calley robots picking up oriental human being babies, shooting them, throwing them into ditches, then your little boat moves on. It's a small world after all."

"Search the place," he said to Russell.

He stood staring at the motionless people as Trung and Russell worked.

Russell came back. "Sheriff, you want to come with me?" he said, the formality letting Alex know there was trouble.

"Lavelle," he called. "Stay in here, watch them. You all stay put now," he said to the room. "I want to remember you just as you were."

136

He followed Russell into the hall. "What do we have?"

"Not a thing. Maybe we need a dog."

Alex thought of the faces, the way they'd smoothed into a cold, knowing blankness when he'd appeared, as if he, not they, had materialized from the past, an armed man walking through a village gate.

"Hold the dog for now," he said. "I'll look some more. They're hiding something in here; I can feel it."

He went back into the display room. He was alone. He stood still, studying the place. A counter, a computer developing setup, supply shelves stacked with boxes. The photographs on the walls here were of picturesque parts of the county. An osprey nested on a single piling in the river. A waterman pulling up a crab pot, the pot draped with jellyfish. Alex felt a flash of rage, seeing his own life looted here.

He looked under the counter. Two ledgers, some calculators, office supplies. A bottle of Black Label Scotch, unopened.

He started going through the cartons of supplies on the shelves. Russell, he saw, had spot-checked a few. From somewhere he heard the sound of a kitten mewling. The animal sounded sick, starved. He opened a box marked *Fujicolor*. Plastic-sealed canisters of film. The next carton was filled with unopened yellow and black boxes of film. Agfa. Kodacolor. He went through every carton. Nothing but film. The sound of the mewling grew more insistent, panicky, as if the cat were walled in somewhere. Maybe it was a baby. From the other room he heard the whisper of voices. Maybe it was Kiet. Trapped. Waiting for his rescue. His elbow brushed the bottle of Scotch and he caught it before it fell. He picked up a metal canister, broke the plastic seal. Unscrewed the top. Poked his finger in, his skin anticipating the grit of the powder. Nothing but film. Where are your young men, the tunnels under your floor? He pulled out the strip savagely.

The mewling rose once more, then trailed into a series of almost human whimpers. He followed the sound to the darkroom door. "Hey!" he heard Russell yell. Minh was suddenly in front of him, blocking the door, the impassive mask at last dissolved into an expression of fear so naked it made Alex turn away. Russell came hurrying after him. Alex motioned him back. "It's OK," he said. "Check the rest of them out; I'm pretty sure there's warrants on some of them—or at least a lack of green cards. I'll take Minh myself, meet you at the station."

"Are you all right?"

"No more than usual."

Alex pushed Minh aside. When he opened the door, the sound stopped. He pushed the light switch. Red light filled the room. The equipment and shelving gleamed dully in it, bulked and misshapen with shadow. Hanging film strips brushed his face like dry fingers. He caught one in his hand. More Vietnamese faces stared at him, their smallness on the film strips making them seem internal, stirring, developing in a black chemical inside himself. There was a strong smell of shit and piss coming from under the aluminum sink. The red and black faces on the negatives, mouths open, were mewling at Alex, a half human cry that pushed on the inside of his skull. "No, please," Minh whispered. Alex opened the door under the sink. The smell drove him back, his eyes stinging. He began to swear, softly but continuously, the spill of curses from his lips flowing into the mewling. The idea came to him, fear knifing into his chest, that this was Kiet, that Minh had Kiet in there. He pulled the heavy door completely open, feeling the handle wet between his fingers. The figure developed in front of his eyes. It was naked, a girl or woman as far as he could tell, though the hairless lips of the sex, exposed between frogged open legs, like all the other crevices and openings were melted together, the wash of napalm or dioxin, he'd seen it before, all the mouths of the body sealed, waxing its scream. Skin ridged and cracked, nipples ripped to the side and smeared down the chest, one arm gone and tied off in a balloon-like stump, the other with a tiny webbed claw at its end. Lips gone, chin melted into chest, one eye melted into something suppurated and bubbling, the other, worse, open and staring at him and now the mouth also and the teeth clicking like mandibles. He wanted to shut the door on it, this thing carved by war, this clay misshapen at the hands of a maniac: the work of his own terrible hands.

"Please," Minh whispered. "It's frightened."

The idea that this was Kiet, even as he knew it couldn't be, still churned panic in his stomach. But when he looked again, the light had shifted or he saw more clearly in it now and the melted woman smoothed back into the past and what he was looking at was a yellow puppy, scared and filthy but unscarred. Above the cabinet he saw another fastened photo, a girl, a napalm victim.

He turned, shaken at the tricks of his mind, the crust of curses that had been left behind his eyelids. He grabbed Minh's collar and twisted. "Tell me where Kiet is. Tell me or I'll kill you."

"No VC here, man," Minh giggled. Alex slowly released him. The dog whimpered.

"Why the hell did you put her in there?"

Minh's eyes widened as if in surprise at the question, the obviousness of the answer. "Because of you," he said. He bent down and picked it up, cradled it to his chest. "What will happen to her if you take me?" He rocked the animal, crooning, his eyes half-closed. "What will happen to her?" The dog whimpered softly. Minh nodded at Alex. "Take her," he commanded. "You take care of her." He thrust the dog at Alex.

Alex reached over and stroked it. Its skin was loose and cool and smooth as human skin under his fingers. "She's a golden child," Minh muttered, and Alex looked at him, not sure if it were Kiet or the dog or what he was referring to. "Half-Vietnamese, half-*My*. American," he explained. "M-Y."

"All mine," Alex said.

Louise was already at work when he got home on Tuesday. He fed the dog some leftover coldcuts. Maybe he'd give it to Baxter. He made a pot of coffee, then poured a cup, poured a slug of

Jameson's into the coffee. He sat at the kitchen table. The weight of the dog pressed warmly against his leg. There was a note Louise had left yesterday, on the bulletin board near the telephone: *Alex, Russell called and said a girl answering to Kiet's description has been spotted in the Point Lookout area again. Alex, are you OK????*

He went out to the barn. It was dark inside, only dimly, moonlit through the windows, and Alex heard mice scurry away as he walked inside. The light fell on his father's old axe. It leaned against a wall, its handle broken, and he remembered the swing of it in his father's hands, the motion frozen in the shape of the old tool. An old Montgomery Ward five horsepower boat motor was clamped to the workbench, the cold, vinegary smell of undrained gas coming from it. The second hand light forced attention, woke the objects from the niches of his memory.

He lit the kerosene space heater and stood up, blinking from the fumes. The rear wall of the studio was mostly glass, double-paned Anderson storm windows that faced out to a meadow and a wall of forest. It was all blackness outside now.

He had taken to working in here at dusk over the last days, the lengthening shadows of trees flowing into the room, touching the raw clay and unshaped stones on the tables and floor, elongating them, widening them, tormenting him as if he were stone, something that had to be born, trapped heavy and inert inside himself. When he flicked on the lights now, the shadows sprang in the other direction, spearing out of the windows, black speared into black.

He unveiled the form and touched it lightly, running his fingers over the swells and dips letting his hands see before his eyes, feeling a tingle on his fingertips. He wet the clay down and touched its sudden dampness and looked for the photograph of Kiet he'd tacked up near the window. But it was gone. Instead his eye fell on his badge and holster, hanging on its peg, then a photograph of himself, in his helicopter—why did he keep it? He closed his eyes, his fingers kneading the clay frantically, mercilessly, pulling the shape out from someplace inside himself.

He opened his eyes. He was staring out of the studio window. For a second he thought he saw the face he was creating under his fingers form in the darkness outside, emerging from leaves even as it was emerging now from the clay. He waited for a moment, but the face didn't disappear. Its white blur against the blackness of the trees configured slowly, inevitably, into upturned eyes, the secret child still waiting in the night, the golden child.

He covered the clay and moved slowly and softly across the room, as cautiously as if he were trying not to wake himself from a dream. He turned off the light. There's nothing there, he told himself. He went out through the side door. He was just going into the house when he heard a loud crack, glass shattering. Footsteps. He ran back. The clay figure was on the grass—it had been thrown through the studio window. Clawed and gouged.

His holster was empty.

"Kiet!" he screamed.

The moon was going in and out of the clouds, doing old ambush tricks. Bushes elongated, changed shapes suggestively, moved in the corner of his vision. A shadow flitted away from the house. What he had chased had followed him. He saw the shadow merge into the shadow of a tree. He yelled the girl's name again.

They were moving into the woods now. He strained to hear under the whistle in his ear. The footsteps seemed to run out from him in different directions. He saw a dark form, flitting between the trees. Then another. The noise stopped. He took a deep breath. He heard something at the end of his exhale, tagged on. A light padding, slow and then faster.

He turned right and ran to the small stream that meandered north and south through the area he was cutting across. He knew where she was going. The thought sickened him. But if he crossed here, he might get in front of her, get to the house before she did. He plunged into the water. As soon as he did, as if he'd displaced it, he sensed something cold and amorphous, a presence that wasn't Kiet, rising behind him, touching the back of his neck. He refused to turn. The things of that country staining into the things of his country. *Noi*, a voice said, another Vietnamese word churned out of his memory: the irresistible urge to drown that seized the kin of the drowned.

He pulled himself out of the water and entered the woods again, staying along the banks of the stream. Something pale rose from a knot of darkness a few feet away from him. It thickened into a figure motioning him, drawing him. He felt without substance, his weight leached off into the darkness. The figure stood directly in front of him—the girl? The woman in the paddy? An old man?—But somehow he saw it as if peripherally. His memory pasting sounds, images on the darkness, that was all. He looked down and saw his hands had disappeared, the stumps of his wrists elongated into shadow.

He picked up his pace and suddenly was out of the trees, into the unprotected openness of a moonlit field. He could see the house on the other side of the field, dark. But strips of light leaked from the spaces between the boards in the barn.

He walked quickly across the field, his breath white and phosphorescent. What the hell would he do with her? The thought of bringing her in, turning her back to Louise, to the group home, among people who had no historical references, seemed absurd. To be counselled. This VC. To con whose soul? He moved to the house. The first window was open. He peered inside. The moonlight was bright enough to make it almost like looking through a starlite nightscope. The objects inside had a two-dimensional, representative look. The room was nearly empty, suggestive with shadow, as if the house was only the half-formed idea of a house. What furniture there was had been draped with sheets. It looked like one of the summer people's houses, shut up for the season, existing in a kind of half-life until its occupants returned. As if Johns had been haunting his own house.

He walked slowly to the barn. Maybe she'd gone there first, hidden. Tobacco spears hung down from the rafters and packing forms lined one wall. The air was thick and dry and acrid. Inside the tool locker that stood near the forms he could see a chainsaw, shovels, a trimming knife, baling wire. Three shotguns and a Winchester lever-action rifle displayed in a rack. An old wood and leather trunk, its hasp held by a rusty lock. He yanked at the lock. It was open. He shuddered, back in Minh's again. The top of the trunk creaked loudly and theatrically as he pulled it up. The smell that blasted out made his eyes sting. Four dead mice, eviscerated, were stuck in each corner. Two dried husks, like blackened and furred banana peels, lay half-curled on top of a mass of wet and matted papers, rusted springs, bolts, screws, tangles of wire, rotting string. He stroked them. Rabbit ears. Nesting material, he figured: junk to give the tobacco forms false weight. He reached inside and began pulling out papers, feeling he was reaching into something alive, Johns' cluttered brain. Internet printout porn, stained photos clipped from magazines: naked adults rubbing against naked children: the men's faces sucked dry, caved in around lips grim pressed with need. Gothic letters, German or Scandinavian, little "O's" cancelled like sewn mouths. Many exclamation points. French: *Les Enfants Terribles De L'Orient.* Some crumpled Polaroids.. He smoothed one out, another. *Kiet.* The same face that had stared at him from his studio wall, and then from the woods outside, cracked and smudged, the slight body, rainbow stained along the fold in the print, cringing among stuffed bears, one hand holding a Raggedy Ann. The terror in the eyes stabbing him. The next picture was worse: the eyes hooded, seductive, a terrible smile, half-blocked by Johns' skinny, hairy ass. He wondered who had taken the photo.

He rubbed his forehead, closed the trunk, shouldered it and brought it out of the barn. He went back inside. The odor of the leaves seemed stronger, something fetid and heavy hanging in the air. A box of matches sat on the workbench. He lit one, tossed it into the tobacco form, into the yaw of the nesting. Did tobacco burn as brightly as thatch? Lighting and dropping matches as he went, he walked back out of the barn.

A shot cracked in the air. He heard glass break, the second time tonight. Three more shots. Something like time spun around in his head. He crouched beneath the window level and worked his way, running, window to window, around to the other side.

A black heap down on the ground under one window. Broken glass glittered on top of it. Behind him there was a dull boom, then crackling; when he turned he could see the flames against the sky, and when he turned back the flickering light painted the man on the ground, revealed and erased and revealed the black hole in the center of Hiram Johns' forehead, the shotgun clutched in his spatulate hand, the twist of surprise on his face.

Alex tried to find a neck pulse, out of politeness. You stupid bastard, he told the farmer. Told himself. Sheriff Minh Trinh Sin. Some sheriff. He stood up and looked through the shattered glass. The room came in flashes, strobed in the reflected dance of light from the burning barn. A kid's room. Four-poster bed, shelves of books and toys. Her room. His trap. He thought of her coming back to the house, finding it empty, except for this room, preserved for her. Waiting. Johns the hunter. Johns the pervert. Both involving a delusional optimism that sometimes worked out. Johns had known she'd run away, knew she'd come back here. But he hadn't known who she was. He hadn't known who owned the night.

As Alex stared inside, his eyes adjusting, he saw the quilt covered shape on the bed.

A chill ran up his neck and scalp. He knew who was under the quilt but for a second he was back in Minh's and he feared what would form in his eyes when he came into the room and uncovered it. He opened the broken window and climbed into the room. She lowered the quilt; he glimpsed his gun, still gripped in her other hand. The fear in her face shivered in his stomach like a kind of grief.

* * *

Smart bombs, *the TV says.*

I hear that, you know what I see, Kiet? See all these bombs with intelligent little faces fall out of the belly of the aircraft, look around, say: no way, and hat off for Canada. Smart bombs. Valedictorian bombs. Ah. Made you laugh.

Whisper shadow, the TV says.

How you get a TV anyway?

A gift, child. From Alex.

He's the tinh *man.*

But I'm not the great and powerful wizard of Oz, child.

Tinh's like a ghost. A soul stealer.

Yes, I remember.

Suck your soul right out of your mouth. Leave you empty and clueless.

Don't be frightened, child. I'm sure he has no designs on you.

—.

Are you still there, child?

Your words put a funny picture in my head. Having designs on me.

I get pictures like that all the time.

I bet you do.

You hungry, child?

Were you always like this?

Do you mean blind or handsome or crazy? Ah, good, another laugh. How long have you been running, child?

All my fucking life, old man.

That can't be too long then. Less time then I've been blind.

One life's not but fifteen years. My dust life. But I carry my VC Ma's life in me.

Are you sure?

Do you mean if I'm carrying her or if she's VC or if I'm crazy?

Even the lies are true, child, if you know how to listen.

You in the war, right?

A hitherto experimental prototype, *the TV says.*

You in the black part of me, old daddy?
Color, child, is something of an abstract for me.
The splib and the dink, that's me.
Now there are some terms I haven't heard in years.
No collateral damage, *the TV says.*
One of my foster dads taught me. He was there too. A splib in
the Nam. In the war. What did you do, Baxter Daddy? You and the
sheriff? You and the tinh? What did you do in the war, Daddy? Tell
me.

Over there he was my hands. My gun. And I was his eyes. We
were Hallam. A weapon. A Chopper. And what good were his
hands? And what good were my eyes?

I'll be whatever you need, old man. Eyes or hands or weapon.
Just live, child. That's all you need do.

It was foggy the next morning, a blankness that blurred the day
Alex saw through his window when he woke up like a chance to
erase the night before, the past, though when he searched
himself for some trace of regret, it just wasn't there. Louise was
next to him; he couldn't remember when she'd come home. They
were entwined, as if their bodies had unconsciously configured
into a memory of the act of love. He didn't know what he would
do now. He let the memory of his actions last night open out
into the light: what he'd done had been insane with its own logic
but led to no ending he could imagine now. He'd had a vision,
seen it like the very form of mercy and tried to claw it out of the
earth and he understood now, lying perfectly still in the white
merciless light of his bedroom, that nothing of the world he
knew would survive that sculpting. Everything around him, the
filtering gauze at the window, the top of his dresser barred with
sunlight, looked normal but somehow hollowed, as if its weight
had been scraped out from under its surface. In the kitchen the
messages scaling the cork bulletin board near the phone seemed
signals from another person's life: dental appointments, notes
about groceries, calls. It all seemed as pathetic as the details of a

life he would notice when he went through the home of a murder or accident victim, appointments and commitments that would never be kept. The row of question marks on Louise's note—Russell's calling about Kiet—still demanded an answer.

The day turned cold, too cold for November: Winter's first breath. That noon, he and Russell drove to the Patuxent in response to a call about a jumper. He stood on the bank of the river, looking up at the Johnson Bridge. It was a beautiful bridge and he could see how putting railings or wire fencing along it would mar the pure white arc of it in the air. Last year when it had been under repair and people had to use a ferry, there had been a sense of isolation, but also of giddy liberation, the county suddenly severed from the road that went over the bridge's arch and north and east, branching off to the state and national capitals.

"Think there's a chance?" Russell asked.

Alex looked down at the search boats skimming in water spider circles under the bridge. He peered at the apex of the arch, the point from which the man had jumped; it was marked by three poles topped with red aircraft warning lights. He shrugged. "Some survive."

"Listen," Russell said. "It's not like you make a habit of shooting the neighbors. Johns must have felt trapped when you showed up to check the house, gone for you. Hell, he had rounds chambered already, his safety off."

"Two out of six last year," Alex said. "They screwed it up somehow. Their jump."

Russell stared at him.

"He was unbalanced, Alex."

"Go ahead," he said to Russell. "I'll wrap things up here."

Russell cocked his head. "You were one of your own deputies, you'd be taking a mandatory stand-down now, Alex."

"R.H.I.P.," Alex said.

He watched Russell walk slowly away and get into his car,

still looking back. He waved once. When the car was gone, Alex started walking up the spine of the bridge. Rising into the air over the river, into an atmosphere tagged to the shore, the earth, but different, full of breezes and touches and whispers. At the apex he stood looking down at the water. He thought about how it must have been, the jumper standing here, and then just stepping out, twisting right off the stem of his life. King Kong staring at the confusion of sharp angles and lights, the terrible complex symmetry of civilization. The ape couldn't adjust to life in New York. In the World. You couldn't take the jungle out of the gorilla. Alex looked out at the World, trying to imagine his place in it. *It's not ours anymore.* The line was from a story, Hemingway; he couldn't recall the context. Or the line was the context. In the newer version of King Kong they'd had the ape go up the World Trade Center instead of the Empire State Building. King Kong, a college English teacher once told him, had all the attributes of the classic tragic hero: of noble birth, had a tragic flaw for tiny blondes, fell from a great height. Alex put his right foot up on the low concrete wall, grasped the pole, pulled himself up. He waved back the deputies beyond the yellow ribbon barriers, smiled at them. Would the apex of an arch bridge over the Patuxent be a great enough height? Would there be a moment of self-discovery before the ape stepped out? Before the climatic splat. Discuss, in five hundred words, the difference between tragic and pathetic.

He let go of the pole, tottered for a second. Unbalanced.

He thought of Kiet, of Louise, as if they were the points in the classic triangle, as if he were engaged in a strange infidelity. How could it go on so long? He felt like the last of something, alone up here on this bridge in the first year of the final decade of the blood-soaked century, in the third century of his blood in this place, at the beginning of a war called as if to finally bring his war to an end. Balanced in the usual position, between pain and oblivion. He stared down at the wrinkling water and pulled a vision up to himself, as if he were a Piscataway, as if out of his own dreams: the rotor wash again parting the rice stalks to reveal the woman he'd once shot, not a dream but a flash in the corner of his eye, like a photo suddenly glimpsed in a wink of light: the squat, the wide eyes, the curve of pregnancy, the terror, his obscene *legerdemain*: the hand quicker than the eye, quick to pull the trigger and not quick enough to jerk up the barrel. The flash burning her into his brain. Only he didn't think she had been, not then. She had just slipped into the long slide of the war that weeks later took him, as if in inevitable progression, over a ditch where he hovered and balanced above the murdering with no other comment than a curse; it was what you were supposed to do; she wasn't the first, she wouldn't be the last; he was just a kid. But she'd come back to him, followed him in a girl to the places of his childhood and ancestry and legacy.

He tried to think of the last week now, last night, see clearly what he'd become involved in, but what he saw now, what his mind spun into a truth more real than memory, was the woman grasping her thighs open as she sank, pulling her belly open, her fingers slipping into the bullet holes and yanking apart her flesh and the newborn neverborn baby bobbing triumphant from the brown water, netted in blood and slime, the baby he'd yanked out of the world before it was born, a birth pulled out of his pain and need, like the movie massacre Kiet had made into a memory of her own, a construct born of pure need and pure truth, as real now to her as the massacre he'd hovered over helplessly, as the image that flared in his mind now, the way Baxter's screen had flared into memory, the way Minh's photos had burst into life: the woman's fingers opening, relinquishing, as she sank under the brown paddy water, the golden child's face emerging.

His heart aching, he could picture Kiet now, forming to her image in his mind, as she had formed trembling from the leaves outside his studio window, from his clay.

And looking down at the vibrant skin of light on the river now, hung balanced over that line at an altitude of fifteen hundred feet, he saw the water become a membrane quivering over the still quivering dead and dying in the ditch; he saw clearly how they hadn't been quite real from his height, the woman he'd shot, the child who'd crawled from that opening in the earth, born from the dead and flung back to them, *tous les enfants terribles de l'orient;* they all hadn't been quite real to him then, the way a nineteen year old's concept of his own death isn't real to himself, but every year since, like a father watching his child growing into its flesh and form as the father grew into his own adulthood, he had grown as responsible for both dead children as if they were one living child, as if he'd casually fathered it when he was nineteen and flown on, as if his bullets were seed, and now the child had become real and had come now into its life and his life in this place, and had become, out of all the memories and nightmares from which he might have chosen, the tag on which he'd hung his life, the way in which he would move as a human being in the world.

It wasn't until late afternoon that he could drive back out to Baxter's. On impulse, he left the car about a quarter mile out and walked in. The ground was soft and wet under a thin dusting of frost. He floundered through the mud, its weight clinging to his legs, slowing him as if he was running from an enemy in a dream. His breath sparkled in the air.

He made a half-circle around the house. At the side he stopped and leaned against the wall and pressed his face to the window. His breath melted the frost on the glass, an eye slowly opening, and in that instant he feared would melt like the frost, he saw Baxter and Kiet sitting next to each other, Kiet's hand resting on Baxter's shoulder. Standing still as if he was frozen, Alex watched, straining to hold the completed shape, the healed circle he'd formed in the world just as it had formed in his mind's eye, his heart. His gloveless hands ached in the cold.

DECEMBER
1994

LIZARD WINE

A RED BANNER WITH yellow slogans on it floated above the trees near a billboard depicting Ho Chi Minh leading the people. Donald Barnes, the Remains Team leader, pointed at another billboard pasted with advertisements in English for condo sales, a tennis club at Hanoi's West Lake. "Makes you wonder what that was all about, don't it?" Barnes nudged Brian. "All that shouting and shooting and running about we did. Isn't that right Comrade Cam?"

Dao Thi Cam, the interpreter, shrugged, said nothing.

Brian rolled down the window. Bicycles and scooters swarmed the car, their horns beeping constantly. The air smelled of mold and old stone and charcoal and gasoline. A taste of bile came into his mouth, like the memory of fear. Vietnam enveloped him again. The Celica passed into a maze of narrow, dusty, tree-shaded streets clogged with vehicles and people, a jumble in his eyes of stalls hung thick with utensils or clothing, rusting iron balconies, crumbling tile roofs, stained cement walls, buildings pressing tightly against each other, every inch taken, used. Cone hatted women squatted on the sidewalks, cooking skewers of meat over glowing braziers, the charcoal smoke twisting up into the air. Boxed television sets, CD's and VCR's were stacked high in front of some shops, the parts of a motorscooter were laid out, dissected, on the sidewalk. Through a cave-like door he saw a row of young men sitting on stools before TV screens, playing kick, punch and dismember video games, their thumbs dancing over the control pads in their hands.

A building complex was being torn down on the next block. "Hanoi Hilton," Barnes nodded, tapping his shoulder. Brian had heard the famous prison was being destroyed, but he wondered if Barnes had just picked this site to see his reaction; the bald, silver-bearded man was grinning at him goatishly. There seemed to be buildings being dismembered on every street they passed anyway, a deconstruction of the city that freed a stinging white dust; it clung to the leaves of the trees, the sidewalks and walls, to Brian's skin now, like the stubborn past. He looked at Dao Thi Cam; she was staring out of the window also. Barnes had told him she was a People's Army veteran; he wondered if she in any way shared his feelings, still saw her city filtered through the dust of the war. But she remained silent.

They parked on a street lined with noodle soup shops. A beggar approached Brian as soon as he left the car, a wizened old lady, her mouth stained with betel nut, her hand extended. Dao Thi Cam put some *dong* in it. It was dusk now and cold; the breaths of the patrons wove white wisps into the steam from the bowls of *pho* they held close to their chins as they shoveled quickly with their chopsticks.

The restaurant Barnes led them to was upstairs and upscale, with French impressionist prints on the walls, white linen table cloths, sleek waiters in white jackets. A small plastic Christmas tree, hung with bulbs, stood on one table: Brian remembered, startled, that it was two days before the holiday. "We're a little early," Barnes said, sitting at a table. Dao Thi Cam sat at the opposite end, nodded slightly to Brian, then closed her eyes, raised two stubby brown fingers as if to make a point, and rubbed at her temples.

"You're a quiet man, Schulman," Barnes said. "You deep in the throes of nostalgia? Having the obligatory flashback?"

"Don's just jealous because he never had a flashback of his own," a tall young man said, walking in, nodding to Brian, then shaking his hand. He had a cropped-side haircut and a pressed denim shirt and pressed jeans and may as well have been in uniform. "He feels unfairly denied."

"The young Captain Wilkes," Barnes said. "Merry Christmas, young captain."

"Welcome to Vietnam," Wilkes said.

"A phrase I'll lay he's heard before." Barnes winked at Brian. "This, young captain, is Dr. Brian Schulman. Doctor Schulman. If this was a squad, we'd call him 'Doc'. Doc's gonna make his bones for us, that right, Doc?"

"That's a phrase I don't understand," Dao Thi Cam said, opening her eyes. "I've never understood it. Making his bones."

Wilkes said something in Vietnamese to her. She seemed not to hear it.

"We're an enigmatic people, us Occidentals," Barnes said. "It's an old Mafia saying, Cam. Means, have you killed someone for the godfather yet?"

"We kill nobody. We're a team for reconciliation," she said bitterly.

"I meant it ironically, Miss Cam. Bones. As in, what we hunt for. We're an ironic and enigmatic people. And Schulman here is, so I've been told, the most formidable of us. He's the bone man. He'll help us succeed where all others have failed."

Brian thought about the bones he'd made at his last dig, the mini-ball and bayonet splintered skeletons of Confederate Civil War prisoners he'd unearthed near the Potomac. He thought of Mary. She had hated the idea of him coming here. He missed her, understood her, felt his wife and son becoming a dream in this place.

"You need to get to know us now, don't you, Miss Cam," Barnes said. "Our nuances and subtleties. It's the program now. It's in the national interest."

"One way or another, it always has been," Dao Thi Cam said. "Trying to know you."

"During the war," Wilkes said to Brian, "she carried copies of Jack London and Hemingway in her knapsack."

Barnes raised his glass to Dao Thi Cam, "Picture it: our enigmatic and ironic Miss Cam, laying there nights on the Ho Chi Minh Trail, trying to figure out what in the world happened, wondering why in the hell those guys with the sled dogs she'd read about were now dropping all this firepower on her head. Wondering where in the hell was Roberto Jordan."

"During the war," Wilkes insisted, frowning at Barnes, "they had guys who came around, lectured units on American literature. To get to know us. I find that remarkable."

"You find that remarkable, do you young captain?" Barnes said.

"Yes, I do; I don't care what you say. Do you think we ever had that certainty about our cause—that we could allow ourselves to see the people we were supposed to kill that clearly?"

"What do you mean 'we,' kemosabe?" Barnes asked.

Brian saw Wilkes glance at Dao Thi Cam quickly, as if to register the effect of his words, the sensitivity he was displaying in contrast to Barnes' coarseness. It was the kind of sexual maneuvering you'd see on any dig; it made Brian feel at home.

"And what about you, Dr. Schulman?" Dao Thi Cam said, ignoring Wilkes. "Do you find us remarkable also? What brings you here, to make your bones?"

"You must already know my credentials."

"Yes. And I've read about your Civil War. It was something else I read, along with Jack London and Hemingway," she said, nodding to Wilkes. "There were six hundred thousand Americans killed in your Civil War, weren't there? A respectable number."

"That's an odd way to put it."

"Did you know that we had three hundred thousand missing? And four million dead? There are many bones to be made here. Dr. Schulman. But of course we limit ourselves to white men, yes, Mr. Barnes?"

"White or black, brown or yellow, long as they're Americans. We is non-discriminatory, comrade Cam."

"Of course. And during the war, Dr. Schulman," she looked at him, and he stared at her, really for the first time. She must have been in her forties, he thought, but you really couldn't see it until you were close; her face, shifting in the light was ageless, her eyes bright and assessing, her lips full, her skin etched with fine lines around her eyes and mouth; she was beautiful, he thought, with her history. "During the war, Dr. Schulman, did you make any bones then?"

"What did you do in the war, daddy?" Barnes snorted. "The obligatory question. Hang on, boyo, before we get into all that. Before we dig up those particular bones, there's something I want you to try. Ah, here."

More Americans and Vietnamese came into the room, filed over to the table. Barnes introduced Brian. Brian shook hands, the names flying past him, Vietnamese and English merging, in his jet lag, his sleeplessness, his sense of unreality at sitting in the enemy capital. The Americans were young, crew cut, dressed in PX civvies; all of them soldiers assigned to the Remains Team; American soldiers, a generation later, back in Vietnam to find what was left behind of and by his generation. The Vietnamese were older; they in fact were his generation. He looked at them, the obligatory question in his own mind, trying to picture their faces as if circled by gun sights.

"You bring it, Duong?" Barnes asked.

"Of course." Duong was wiry, his forearms corded and scarred. Hard-core, Brian thought. He had a thin, tough face and stained teeth. He was smoking. All the Vietnamese were smoking. "Yes, of course." He put several ceramic bottles on the table. The waiter came immediately and placed glasses in front of each person. Brian suspected a ceremony.

"Nguyen Thinh Duong," Barnes introduced him again. "And what he has there is lizard wine. Wine of the lizard that bit you. To bid you welcome back." He winked at Brian. "An odd way to put it, right?"

"Lizard wine?"

"Scales of the dragon that bit you. I know—you're hoping for some kind of metaphor, right? Like Red Dog beer, they don't pickle this red dog, eviscerate him, let his blood and entrails soak into the hops, let his body float in the bottle. But no such luck, Doc; lizard wine ain't no metaphor. Nary a metaphor in it. Only a literal lizard. And we wonder why they won the war. Better you can't see it, partner." He tapped one of the ceramic bottles. There were Chinese letters embossed on it. "Think tequila. Think of the worm. And be thankful this isn't glass." He picked it up and poured it into Brian's glass, his own, Nguyen Thinh Duong's. Passed it around the table.

"To your bones, Doc," he said, and drank. Brian raised the glass and drank also. It wasn't bad; sake-like, perhaps stronger. He felt its warmth spreading through him with surprising speed. Into his bones.

The others at the table echoed the toast.

Brian watched Dao Thi Cam drink, her throat moving under her skin. Everything was suddenly clearer. Something pulsed at his temples, in his groin. Vietnam, he thought again, as if he had to name it to pin the reality of his being here. The waiter was putting down little dishes of cucumber salads. Dao Thi Cam smiled slightly.

"You drink like a soldier."

"We're all soldiers here, Miss Cam," Barnes said.

"Dr. Schulman also? I asked what you did during the war, Dr. Schulman."

"Brian."

"Then you must call me Cam."

"Cam." Last name first in Vietnamese, he remembered. He shrugged. "I was aircrew during the war, Cam. Helicopters. Though I spent some time on the ground also. Mostly in Quang Ngai, Quang Nam and Quang Tri provinces."

Duong looked at him. "I was in those provinces also," he said. "In mortars."

We're all soldiers here. A ditty sung in Quang Ngai or Quang Nam or Quang Tri province twenty-five Christmas eves before went through Brian's head: *Jingle-bells /Mortar shells/VC in the grass/You can take your Christmas truce/And shove it up your ass.* Who am I drinking with, here in Hanoi? he thought. "Then we have something in common."

"Were you a mortarman also?

"No, but I was mortared." Duong laughed. Brian clicked glasses with him. "I'm happy sir, that you missed me."

Duong grinned. "And I am happy also, sir, that your airplane did not see me."

"What does it mean," Cam said, "to be aircrew?" She wasn't smiling. "What did you do?"

"We observed," he said. And sometimes, he thought, we brought things down. On that which we observed. Sometimes we made our bones. She stared at his face, their eyes locked across the table. "I hated your airplanes," she said. "The B-52's, as Duong said. But all of them. The jets. The helicopters. They killed everything. Everything on the ground. And sometimes they came down. I hated that the most."

Her eyes were hard, unforgiving.

"I hated that too, when they came down," he said, trying to lighten it and Duong laughed, shaking his head at Cam, but she didn't smile. She was staring at him, and suddenly he was glad, glad for her implacability. He took another drink.

"Do you remember?" Barnes said, "how we used to bullshit during the war, how one day we'd all sit around and blow weed with the VC? It was just one of those things you'd say, right?" He poured more lizard wine.

"I would try to imagine," Cam said, "your faces. The aircrew. But you were just noise. Noise above us and the leaves and the trees shivering. Noise and terror. I tried. But I couldn't make myself believe anything in those machines had human faces."

He drank the wine, looking at her face. The warmth had turned into heat now, pushing through his veins, under his skin. He looked at the kids at the other end of the table, young American faces, flesh growing as he watched over the bones he was here to find; he'd seen enough of them too, in his aircraft, on the ground. Their human faces, rotting into the ground now. Something hardened inside him. "What did you do," he asked her. "In the war?"

She shook her head.

"She was in the Youth Volunteers," Duong said. "Do you know what they were?"

"They were these kids," Barnes said. For a moment Brian saw him look around the table, the young American soldiers silent, looking at them. "High school kids from Hanoi, fifteen, sixteen, seventeen years old. They used them on the Ho Chi Minh Trail, to repair the bomb damage, defuse the unexploded bombs. Sappers. But a lot of them were just these kids, these teenage girls like Cam."

He tried to picture it, picture her. "How?" he said to her.

"I don't understand."

"How did you do it? Repair the bomb damage."

"It was where I learned to dig. A skill that has become useful now, yes? We worked in small teams, like this one. Each was responsible for each kilometer of trail. If there were unexploded bombs, we'd try to disarm them, but if we couldn't we'd dig holes around them, until we could make them, how do you say? Vertical. Then they'd be exploded. And those craters and all the craters from your bombs, we'd fill in."

"How?" he asked, needing to see it, to know the details of it.

"Mostly, we used our hands. Many of us died, doing that. You'd come often, while we did that. Your aircraft. Your aircrews."

He saw an army of women, moving under the trees into which he'd fired, erasing the war as they went. "Sometimes we flew over the Trail, shot down." Brian said to her, nodding, wanting to drink it in like the wine, her hatred, her condemnation, the shadows of his having touched this place at all. "It was all triple canopy around there: we could never see you." He looked at her face across the table. She was staring at him also. She looked away.

"Did you know there's groups of vets," Barnes said, "come

back here now, go down to the places they fought? Looking for some sort of geographic closure or something. How about you, Doc? You ever feel a need for a little geographic closure? On a personal level?"

Brian thought of a friend, Alex Hallam, also ex-aircrew, who'd adopted a girl born in this country under the mist, taking her into his home as if he had wanted to pull her into the hatch of his aircraft. Closure, Mary had said. Brian realized how much he hated the word. "I'm an archaeologist and a forensic anthropologist; I don't really believe in closure," he said. "Whatever's been covered can always be uncovered, or sometimes even uncovers itself, works its way out of the earth. Whether you want it to or not."

"Sure as hell would make our lives easier," Barnes said. "Little thingies working their own way out."

"Hey, you know?" one of the young soldiers said, his voice drunk, his face still the resentful face of a dead GI Brian had carried on his helicopter, "Fuck all you old guys. Make us spend our Christmas at your damn war."

"Exactly. Fuck all us old guys," Duong nodded, shaking his head at Cam.

"Yes," Cam said dully. "We must look to the future. To a future of prosperity for all. Hooray for the future. We must bury the past. The past is just a rotten nail in our heads. We must bury the past by digging up the past, yes, Mr. Schulman? We must extract the last of you, Doctor Archaeologist-Aircrew, and send you home."

"Listen," Barnes said. "It's time to play the drinking game. FNG's the captain. Right?"

Brian had played it before, on other digs, with other archaeologists, with soldiers. Now he was the captain. The Fucking New Guy. Glasses were filled to the brim, each in turn drained; if someone didn't do it, Brian had to drink the filled glass. Cam drank one glass, then refused another. She watched him with what he thought was amusement; she was the kind of woman who liked, he thought, to sit and be in control, to watch others lose it. "Good for the male strength," Duong tapped the bottle as he filled Brian's glass, and Brian felt the heat, a lizard stir in his groin. Cam sneered at him. He felt a flush of shame, then emptiness, a twist of grief, the lizard moving up, gnawing at his entrails. I insist, I insist, Duong grinned at him. Come on, Doc, drink, he heard Barnes command, as if from a distance, and he felt the heat of the wine swirl into his throat, his head, his veins.

Barnes had filled Duong's glass again. Everybody was staring at him. Duong looked at the wine, then at Brian. What seemed to be small silver scales floated in the liquid. The table was suddenly quiet. Brian saw Cam looking at Duong with concern. He saw Duong's eyes were swimming with distress. "Please," he said to Brian.

"No way," Brian said. "I'm your captain. It's an order. I insist."

Duong's face twitched. He brought a broken-nailed finger up and tapped the glass, then his forehead. "Quang Tri," he said to Brian, naming, Brian understood, what the wine was opening in his head, the hot rubber blackness of a night in Quang Tri, split by flares and tracers, riven with screams, and he nodded and reached over and took Duong's glass and drained it, took it away from Duong and into himself.

He was still drunk when they brought him to the hotel, a narrow six story Graham Greene affair of sooty concrete and iron balconies, a circle with Chinese ideograms carved into the stone wall in front. The room had a cot-sized bed, a desk and armoire of carved black wood. He lay down on the bed and stared at the high ceiling, listening to the Vietnamese voices drifting into the grated window. A dog barked. The ceiling spun. The voices merged into a dream; he was trying to teach a class of archaeology students how to read Vietnamese, writing words whose meaning he didn't know on the black board and pretending to the class he knew what they meant, making it up

162

as he went along. He heard a bang in the dream and then he was awake, looking at the door. He was sure he'd heard it open. Or close. He saw a shadow, suddenly, briefly, in the squares of frosted glass that formed the top half of his door, but when he tried to rise, he groaned, and lay back down. He turned his head sideways on the pillow, wet with his drool. There was a jar—he was sure it hadn't been there before—on the small desk. A note was propped against it. *To Dr. Schulman, Aircrew. With fond memories, and a happy Christmas. Welcome back. Your ghost, Cam.* He picked up the jar—it was plastic, not glass—feeling the heavy shift of the liquid in it. A little of the wine sloshed from the top, cold on his skin, its smell turning in his stomach. The lizard was gutted open, its head swollen with absorbed alcohol, its split body winged out, the ragged edges of its entrails and skin tattered and waving in the current awakened by Brian's lifting. Floating in the dark liquid it seemed on the very edge of liquidity and dissolution, the leather of it on the verge of sea change. Yet its form, flat-eyed, hunched and predatory, remained intact and snarling, held softly in a scale-flecked liquid darkness into which it refused to dissolve, rigid but curled and fetal all at once, something terrible and dead that contained in the very shape of its death the coiled threat of rebirth.

The site they were to dig was on an island in Halong Bay, northeast of Hanoi. The airplane, an F-105 out of Thailand on one of the early bombing missions, had been hit and crashed into one of the three thousand islands that formed an archipelago across the bay. Even though the crash site was known to the Vietnamese, the pilot's body had never been recovered and until the new normalization agreements, they hadn't allowed an American team to the crash scene. Nam Hien, the man who was to meet the team in the town of Hong Gai, on Halong Bay, had been in charge of the antiaircraft battery that had brought the plane down. He would guide them to the site.

They drove to Haiphong, took the ferry over to Quang Ninh and then journeyed through a landscape of jade paddies and mountains that looked like the war. They were to meet Nam Hien and the other members of the team in the banquet room of the tourist hotel where the search team was booked. It was Christmas eve. In the lobby, several young men were sitting around a television, watching a music video and singing karaoke into a microphone, a small plastic Christmas tree set up on the table next to them. A photograph of Ho Chi Minh and a red star decorated the wall behind the banquet table.

Nam Hien was a stocky, dark man with bright eyes and a strong grip, something Brian noticed first when they met and shook hands, and later during the meal and the inevitable drinking bout after it, when he kept clutching Brian's arm spasmodically and painfully whenever he'd tell a story or direct Brian to a new item of food. It was a grip that seemed either deliberately punishing or as if he needed to test Brian's reality. Quang Ngai, Quang Nam and Quang Tri, Brian said. Then Nam Hien told Brian where he had been in the war. Brian made the joke about being glad he'd missed him. *We're all soldiers here.* They ate blood oysters and shrimp cakes with the whole shrimps embedded in them and drank bottle after bottle of Heineken and Tiger beer. As if they had to get someplace else together, Brian thought. As if they had to become new stories to each other.

I'll tell you a story, Nam Hien said, nodding, Cam translating his words to Brian. His unit had been the first to shoot down an American plane. Their antiaircraft gun had been located next to the building where they sat now. "Not this building," Cam interjected. "Most of this city was destroyed during the war, by your bombing." Right here, Hien insisted, gripping Brian's arm hard. An A-7, was that right? The pilot had ejected. Fallen into the Bay. They'd jumped into a boat and raced out to him. Raced against all the fishing boats and sampans trying to get to him first. The soldiers were afraid the fishermen would kill him. And in fact the fishermen got to the spot first. There was only the white silk top of the chute floating in the water. The fishermen grabbed it and hauled the pilot up, but as soon as he broke the surface they began beating him with sticks and gaffing hooks. Pushing him back under. Hien and his men yelled at them, then Hien went over the side. He grabbed the pilot as he was sliding under, pulled him back to the surface. The front of the man's flight suit was ripped open and Hien remembered being startled, seeing nothing but a coarse mat of wet, black body hair. Thinking, in that instant, as if to comfort himself: *you see, it is true, they are not us, they are beasts.* The American was sinking, both his arms broken, and when Hien gripped him, he screamed. Hien could see it under the water, see the silver bubble escape the pilot's mouth. But he held on, gripped the pilot's arm tightly and drew him back to the surface, he said, his hand reaching over now and clutching Brian's arm again, his fingers pushing in painfully on Brian's biceps.

They drank. Then they went out into town, Brian and the Vietnamese: the other Americans stayed back in the hotel. All around him people were clustered in small groups, coalescing and branching up paths and beading out up the slope of the steep mountain to which the town clung. Laughing, singing, eating, drinking, shooting off sparklers and firecrackers. Climbing to the bombed out cathedral on top. It was the way people in Hong Gai, a town with no Christians, celebrated Christmas, Cam explained to him. He who shared the same nationality as the men who bombed both the town and the cathedral. Vietnamese people pressed in on all sides of him, their skins warm and damp from the exertion of the climb, the drinking. They stared at him. Most of them were too young to have been in the war, he told himself. Hello, hello, children called. The crowd pressed in on him. A string of fireworks went off in long staccato bursts, the sharp cordite stink mixing with the other smells. A film, shot down fliers paraded before a screaming mob, faces distorted with hate, began to roll through his mind. He thought about Duong, tapping his head, naming what was being set loose in it by the lizard wine.

Someone clutched his right hand. Someone else clutched the other. Duong had come up on his right side, Hien on his left and they gripped his hands tightly, pulling him up the path to the top of the mountain. He could see the city, a broken outline of lights, a jumble of concrete blocks built since the war, laying below them, spread down the slope and on the apron of ground before the bay. He could see the cathedral at the crest, the point of convergence for the crowd, a jagged shell, roofless, a reminder of the war, of a peace that hadn't been built yet. There was an altar at its east wall, people lighting candles and incense in front of it. Hien and Duong held onto his hands tightly, and he held onto theirs, the two of them pulling him out of the dark water into which he had been falling.

They took Christmas day off. Brian slept through most of it, though on the boat the next morning, he still felt queasy and his head throbbed. Hien, standing in the bow, smiled and waved at him, and Duong brought him a cup of bitter green tea, and Cam looked away disdainfully.

The day was misty. The boat glided through a maze of islands, jagged and worn and mossy as bad teeth. He tried to imagine how it would have been, to fly from some carrier or base in Guam or Thailand into the dragon fangs of this weird seascape.

"There!" Hien called.

The boat had emerged from a channel and was coming around the left side of an island, its cliff rising to a peak hundreds of feet above them. At its base were the two black eyes of a cave system, the white rock face around it grooved and ridged as if sculpted. To the right of and just above the cave was a flat shelf, as if a jagged puzzle piece had been removed from below the peak; a copse of trees bristled up from the left side of the shelf. Brian looked back down. A small boat glided past them, a child and a dog playing in front of the thatched shelter in its bow, a woman cooking on a charcoal grill, a cone-hatted fisherman standing at the tiller in the stern, ignoring them. A red flag flew from the top of the shelter. He looked again at the cliff, the cave; he saw a path etched up to its right, into the trees, an echoing red pennant fluttering on the small plateau to mark the site where they would dig.

It took them two hours to get to the top and another hour to set up the sifting trays. The Vietnamese had marked the site already. The starred mark of the impact where the plane had hit was overgrown, but some of the foliage already cut away. At least there was soil there, rocky soil but not solid rock, as he'd first feared. The digging would be difficult but not impossible. He wondered if the area had been partially pulverized by the crash itself. It was possible, he supposed. But if there had been any surface debris from the plane—there had to be, he thought—it had been cleared out long before. He staked out lines for two trenches bisecting the most likely area of impact.

The younger Americans and Vietnamese formed a bucket line, bringing the soil and rocks to the sifting trays he set up on the edge of the site. He and Hien stood side by side, watching the soil as it fell through the wire grid of the tray, looking for any objects that might have been left: bits of metal or singed cloth or, better, anything with a name or part of a name on it, or, best of all, bone. Pieces of Lieutenant Commander Anthony Deramus, once of Mount Vernon, Ohio, survived by a wife, now remarried, and two children, both as old as the kids working for him in this team. Lieutenant Commander Deramus, missing yet perhaps on the verge of being found. But the soil, sand and rock, sifted into nothing, left behind itself only a ghost of white dust that caked their skin.

"Hey doc," Barnes called, "I think we got something."

Brian walked over to the other side of the trench.

"Here," Barnes said, patting.

Brian patted the same area gently. He could feel the cylindrical shape, just under the skin of earth, perfect, too perfect. Was that you, Mr. Deramus? He brushed the earth aside gently, layer by dermic layer, and he could see it now, brown and aged. But too wide. Like the bone of a giant. He started to move down it, further and further, evacuating a little trench on each side of it, but it went on and on, too far, until Duong's hand came down and stopped his, and Duong reached down further in the trench and pulled it all up, a pointed wooden stake, black and brown and soft rotted in places.

"*Hang Dau Go,*" he said. Brian looked at Cam, who had gotten up and was standing next to him, hitting her hands against her thighs.

"The Cave of the Sharpened Stakes," she said dully. "It's on another island, near here. Tran Gung Dao, the emperor. When the Mongols invaded us, he hid many thousands of such stakes on these islands. The Mongols came in a large force. Three hundred thousand. Destroying everything. We let them come. Deep into us. Then we destroyed them."

She turned her face away.

"When?" Brian asked, looking at the stake, trying to date it. A punji stake, he thought. He wondered if the Vietnamese had smeared them with shit then also. When they used them against the Mongols. Only we didn't know about the Mongols, he thought. We didn't know anything.

"Thirteenth Century," Duong said. He started to laugh. He explained the situation rapidly, in Vietnamese and then the others joined in and the Americans also, all of them looking at each other, enjoying the sudden release of tension. But Cam, Brian saw, didn't join them. She'd squatted at the lip of the trench, staring at the weapon that had refused to soften into the earth around it or remain buried, her face clenched with grief and disappointment.

Hien, at one of the sifting trays, called out to Brian. He held up what he'd found, a small white piece of metal. Brian took it, caressing the smoothness, the sharp edges. It was blank, nameless and numberless, but it was their first piece of the plane. He grinned at Hien and nodded. Hien smiled back and spoke rapidly. Brian looked around and saw Cam working in the ditch near him as if nothing had happened, her hands, brown, blunt-fingered, capable, carefully parting the earth. She looked up at him. "Would you mind translating?" he asked.

"He said he was very excited," she said.

"I can see that," Brian smiled. Cam translated.

Hien spoke again. He was no longer smiling.

"No," Cam said. "He's excited at what he's found now also, but he means then. What he found—it made him think of the day they shot the plane down." Hien nodded, spoke more. "He says, they had been bombed a few times, but this time was the first he caught the airplane in his sights. It had dropped its bombs on the town and there was a great noise as houses collapsed. But in it, he says, he was in a kind of cone of silence and there was an instant that he felt, how would you say, glued. No, as if there was a very straight line drawn from inside him, through his eyes and hands to the gun, the plane. He says that he knew in that instant he would hit the plane. And when he did, it twisted up, very slowly, and then slammed down in a straight line, very quickly. He saw it hit."

Hien smiled, said something else softly.

She frowned. "He says, he saw that future clearly. That instant when he would hit the plane. But he never saw this future, that one day he would stand here with an American friend, digging to build a future."

"Don't you share his feelings?"

"To be frank, I think they're exaggerated. For your benefit."

"Why bother?"

"Oh, everybody wants to turn from the war now, turn to the future. To normalcy. To the life they think will come with normal relations, with your power, your money. Though really I think it's more the way of looking at the world they see in you. The freedom to live without ideology or self-sacrifice. But we don't like to think that. It's not sentimental enough."

"No one could accuse you of sentimentality, Cam."

"Oh, most Vietnamese are very sentimental, romantic. How else could we have won against you? But I prefer not to be.

Perhaps I miss ideology and self-sacrifice. Perhaps I remember too many things, Mr. Schulman. Too many things to dig up and then simply bury again. I remember planes like the one that crashed here. Or the bigger ones, the B-52's. Once, I remember; it was our worst time, on the Trails. Near Khe Sanh, where you were. The bombing was so bad, we hadn't had food for a long time. We girls. We were eating roots. Gnawing, that's the word, isn't it? But sharing whatever we had. And sometimes you'd spray the jungle with poison, but we couldn't allow ourselves to care. Our clothes were rotting off our bodies. I remember, once, how these truck drivers stopped, near where we were digging. They were the bravest men, the drivers, and these were the best of them. They wore a kind of, how do you say, armor, helmets and vests, so they looked like mushrooms. We called them mushrooms, those men. In the bombing, they would just keep going, keep driving, even if they were being blown up, one after the other. Because of belief, you see. One of the mushrooms looked at me then, his truck stopped by me, and he forced me to take a tin of meat. He had to force me, because what we had we saved for the fighters and drivers like him, and I was ashamed. But I took it and I sat and ate it very quickly. My stomach holding around each bit like I had a fist inside me. I was so concentrated on that eating that I didn't even pay attention when your planes came, when your bombs fell. I just remember hearing a great noise, outside but also inside my head, like my mind was being ripped in two. And then I woke up and all the trees were gone and all the trucks and men and my friends and I was alone in the middle of a crater and everywhere I could see were craters and everything was silent and my country was gone. So for a while, for days until I found people again, I thought I was alone in the world, that you had finally peeled my country from the earth. That I was a ghost."

She turned from him, her eyes brimming, her mouth set and tough.

Get some, they would say, and cheer when they'd hear the

bombings, Brian remembered, and looking at her he saw it, saw her waking, a young woman utterly alone under the suddenly silent sky where sometimes he would hang.

She squatted next to the trench. Her shoulders, he saw, were trembling. He squatted down next to her, seeing suddenly what she would see in this work he'd felt compelled to take up, this wound he'd ripped into a wound, and then, a part of him thinking she'd find the gesture sentimental or romantic or presumptuous, a part of him not thinking very much at all, he began clawing at the pile of dirt and rock, pulling it back into the trench. "What are you doing?" Duong called to him, and then Hien and the others called out also, Barnes staring at him, but he ignored them and after a while she began to help him, scooping in the rocks and dirt, patting down firmly, filling in what he'd opened in the ground. And he stopped then, and for a moment he stood still and watched her hands smoothing the earth in a motion that passed into him like peace.

About the Author

Called by Tim O'Brien "one of the most gifted writers to emerge from the Vietnam War," Wayne Karlin has written four previous novels: *Crossover, Lost Armies, The Extras* and *Us*, and a memoir, *Rumors and Stones*. In 1995, he co-edited *The Other Side of Heaven: Post War Fiction by Vietnamese and American Writers*, about which the *Asian American Press* said "Veterans from both sides of the war are hailing *The Other Side of Heaven* as a major contribution toward international healing." He is also one of the editors for the Curbstone Press "Voices from Vietnam Series" and edited the first two books in the series, Le Minh Khue's *The Stars, The Earth, The River* and Ho Anh Thai's *Behind the Red Mist*.

The recipient of an NEA fellowship in fiction and four Maryland State Arts Council Individual Artist Awards in fiction, Wayne Karlin lives in St. Mary's City, Maryland.

CURBSTONE PRESS, INC.

is a non-profit publishing house dedicated to literature that reflects a commitment to social change, with an emphasis on contemporary writing from Latino, Latin American and Vietnamese cultures. Curbstone presents writers who give voice to the unheard in a language that goes beyond denunciation to celebrate, honor and teach. Curbstone builds bridges between its writers and the public – from inner-city to rural areas, colleges to community centers, children to adults. Curbstone seeks out the highest aesthetic expression of the dedication to human rights and intercultural understanding: poetry, testimonies, novels, stories, and children's books.

This mission requires more than just producing books. It requires ensuring that as many people as possible know about these books and read them. To achieve this, a large portion of Curbstone's schedule is dedicated to arranging tours and programs for its authors, working with public school and university teachers to enrich curricula, reaching out to underserved audiences by donating books and conducting readings and community programs, and promoting discussion in the media. It is only through these combined efforts that literature can truly make a difference.

Curbstone Press, like all non-profit presses, depends on the support of individuals, foundations, and government agencies to bring you, the reader, works of literary merit and social significance which might not find a place in profit-driven publishing channels, and to bring the authors and their books into communities across the country. Our sincere thanks to the many individuals who support this endeavor and to the following foundations and government agencies: Connecticut Commission on the Arts, Connecticut Arts Endowment Fund, Connecticut Humanities Council, Daphne Seyboldt Culpeper Foundation, J.M. Kaplan Fund, Eric Mathieu King Fund, Lannan Foundation, John D. and Catherine T. MacArthur Foundation, National Endowment for the Arts, Open Society Institute, Puffin Foundation, and the Woodrow Wilson National Fellowship Foundation.

Please support Curbstone's efforts to present the diverse voices and views that make our culture richer. Tax-deductible donations can be made by check or credit card to:
Curbstone Press, 321 Jackson Street, Willimantic, CT 06226
phone: (860) 423-5110   fax: (860) 423-9242
www.curbstone.org

Praise for *Rumors and Stones*

"For the sake of humanity, we need to read Wayne Karlin on war and peace. Studying the holocaust of his immediate forebears and the Viet Nam/American War of his own experience, he has written a life-saving book."—Maxine Hong Kingston

"Karlin's deft melding of disparate narratives will stand as a unique and valuable addition to the literature of the Holocaust."
—*Washington Post Book World*

"A gem of a book burnished with poetic language and images."
—*Baltimore Jewish Times*

"A haunting meditation."—*Publishers Weekly*

"What a story! Wayne Karlin tells of his uncommon journeys to Asia and Poland. Here is the crisp detail and mellow eye of the master storyteller. *Rumors and Stones* is without a doubt his best work."
—Larry Heinemann

"I think that Wayne Karlin has more of a feel and understanding of the language than most poets I know."—Lucille Clifton

"Karlin's literary achievement is a rare amalgam of stylishness and depth, a dramatic search for Jewish roots in a Polish village ravished by the Holocaust that draws originality and power from the large and melancholy mind of its author."—*The Dissident*

"The weakest writing about war and atrocities simply reiterates what we already know, but the best of it illuminates what we need to know and how it must be expressed, which is what this book is about. Karlin is one of our finest writers, and *Rumors and Stones* is the latest evidence of that fact."—George Evans

Praise for *The Other Side of Heaven*

"A superb collection."—*Kirkus Reviews*

"Stunning in both scope and content."—*Publishers Weekly*

"...a powerful short story collection. In the ever expanding ocean of Vietnam War literature, this anthology stands alone."
—Arthur Hirsch, *The Baltimore Sun*

"The Vietnamese writers...will be new to most readers. Writers such as Bao Ninh, Le Luu, Da Ngan, and Nguyen Quang Thieu provide us with powerful work, stories that bring us inside Vietnam and reflect back on a world addicted to war, but also to the search for understanding and for peace."—Donna Seaman, *Booklist*

"Veterans from both sides of the war are hailing *The Other Side of Heaven* as a major contribution toward international healing."
—Frank Joseph, *Asian American Press*

"The book links the triangle of former adversaries to examine not so much the war itself but the effects of the war."
—Ralph Blumenthal, *The New York Times*

"Not only is this a rich anthology of literary value, but it is also a book of healing. *The Other Side of Heaven* stands without peers.
—Jason Zappe, *Copley News Service*

"The editors of *The Other Side of Heaven* have created a dramatic setting for these stories, juxtaposing the Vietnamese and American tales. A kind of dialogue unfolds, often greater than the single stories themselves. Some of the best writing so far about the Vietnam War is contained here."—Michael Stephens, *The Hungry Mind Review*

"...this volume will secure a place as a seminal contribution to the literary understanding of the war and its aftermath."
—*DAV Magazine*